Dear Readers,

I still remember the first time I read Donald Goines, the god-father of street lit. He was the first to write books about characters I could identify with. To some, the stories may have been aggressive, overly stylized, and even dangerous. But there was an honesty there—a realness. I made a vow that if I wrote a book or got into the publishing game, I would try the same one-two punch—that of a Daddy Cool or Black Gangster.

In 2005, my memoir, *From Pieces to Weight*, marked the beginning. Now I'm rounding up some of the top writers, same way I rounded up some of the top rappers in the game, to form **G-Unit** and take this series to the top of the literary world. The stories in the **G-Unit** series are the kinds of dramas me and my crew have been dealing with our whole lives: death, deceit, double-crosses, ultimate loyalty, and total betrayal. It's about our life on the streets, and no one knows it better than us. Not to mention, when it comes to delivering authentic gritty urban stories of the high and low life, our audience expects the best.

That's what we're going to deliver, with such street lit superstars as **K'wan**, bestselling author of *Gangsta* and *Hood Rat*; **Relentless Aaron**, author of *Push* and *The Last Kingpin*; and **Méta Smith**, author of *Queen of Miami* and *The Rolexxx Club*.

You know, I don't do anything halfway, and we're going to take this street lit thing to a whole other level. Are you ready?

G Unit
Books

New York London Toronto Sydney

HEAVEN'S FURY

50 Cent and Méta Smith

G Unit
Books   BOOKS

Pocket Books
A Division of Simon & Schuster, Inc.
1230 Avenue of the Americas, New York, NY 10020

This book is a work of fiction. Names, characters, places, and
incidents ⋯⋯⋯⋯⋯⋯⋯⋯⋯⋯⋯⋯⋯ or are
used fictit⋯⋯⋯⋯⋯⋯ to actual ⋯, ⋯ or ⋯les or
persons, li ⋯ing or dead, is entirely coincidental.

Copyright ⋯⋯⋯⋯⋯⋯ 2007 by G-Unit Books

MTV Music Television and all related titles, logos, and characters are
trademarks of MTV Networks, a division of Viacom International Inc.

All rights reserved, including the right to reproduce this book or
portions thereof in any form whatsoever. For information address
Pocket Books Subsidiary Rights Department, 1230 Avenue of the
Americas, New York, NY 10020

First G-Unit/MTV/Pocket Books trade paperback edition
November 2007

POCKET BOOKS and colophon are registered trademarks of
Simon & Schuster, Inc.

For information about special discounts for bulk purchases,
please contact Simon & Schuster Special Sales at 1-800-456-6798
or business@simonandschuster.com.

Designed by Jaime Kerner-Scott

Manufactured in the United States of America

10   9   8   7   6   5   4   3   2   1

ISBN-13: 978-1-4165-6208-5
ISBN-10:   1-4165-6208-7

Dedicated to the memory of my father,
Jesse Thurman Smith.
I miss you Pretty Smitty.

ACKNOWLEDGMENTS

Thank you, Jesus, for keeping me safe on this journey. I am trying to serve you better.

Thank you, Mom, for helping me so much with everything.

Thank you, Jordan, for sharing your time with my work. You're an awesome kid and Mommy loves you so much.

Thank you, Tyra Martin, for doing so much to help my career and for all the sweet hookups. This year the Emmy is yours! I hope you get that and everything else you deserve.

Thank you, Angela Allen, for all the hospitality, friendship, sisterhood, and everything else you do. Now step up that cake game and make my shoe cake!

ACKNOWLEDGMENTS

Thank you, Young Bizzle, for being a supportive and honest friend (so far . . . lol), for reminding me to pray, for praying with me, and for being the last of the good guys.

Thanks to Ben a.k.a. Hyckef the God for being a character!!! I'm rooting for you . . . and praying for you. Lord have mercy. Haha.

Thanks to Cheri, Dino, Tracey, Landry, and Schun for being amazing friends and for bearing with my nonresponse to emails and phone calls when I'm in the zone.

Thanks to Dawn Michelle of Dream Relations for all you've done.

Thanks to Marc Gerald and Lauren McKenna for the opportunity.

Thanks to Chicago and Gary for holding me down.

A world of gratitude to all the readers, libraries, book clubs, bookstores, and media who have shown their continued support.

Last of all, but absolutely not least, thanks to Curtis "50 Cent" Jackson for allowing me to be a part of G-Unit. Holla at ya girl.

Prologue
HERE COMES THE BRiDE

December 2002, St. Michael the Archangel Catholic Church, Chicago

THE BRIDE LOOKED BEAUTIFUL in her traditional white gown. She twirled in the mirror and grinned at her reflection. She didn't want to seem vain, but she did look really beautiful. She couldn't believe that her wedding day had finally arrived. It was the happiest day of her life. Her mother and grandmother cried tears of joy and the ceremony hadn't even begun; they were just so touched at the pure beauty before them.

"I remember my wedding day," the bride's mother said. "I was so nervous."

"I'm not nervous at all," the bride replied. "I'm too happy to be nervous."

"No jitters about the wedding night?" the grandmother asked with a wicked grin. "Life as a married woman has its . . . duties."

"Abuelita!" the bride said with a giggle. "I'm not nervous about *that*, either."

The grandmother put her hand over her heart. "*Dios mío!* Please tell me that you're not . . . experienced!" The bride's mother and grandmother both waited for her reply. The bride smiled cryptically but didn't answer, and the women's eyes grew wide with shock. Unable to control herself, the bride erupted in a fit of giggles.

"Relax, Abuela. Relax, Mami. I'm pure as the driven snow. I just couldn't help teasing you a little."

"Don't play with us like that," the bride's mother replied, exhaling in relief.

"You know how important it is to God to remain a virgin until you're married," her grandmother said.

"I do."

"And Ricardo, he never pressured you to go all the way?" her mother asked.

"No, Mami. He's a good man. The best," the bride said. "I'm so lucky. Most guys would never have understood how important my faith is to me, but not my Rico. He respects the fact that I'm a virgin. In fact, he told me that he loved me *more* because I was one."

The mother and grandmother of the bride smiled at each other, filled with pride. They'd raised their little girl in the Church, and she didn't stray. That was a difficult feat to achieve in the twenty-first century.

The bride's grandmother took a string of pearls from around her neck and placed them around the bride's.

"Abuela—" the bride began. Her grandmother silenced her.

"*Sí*, your *abuelo* gave me these and now I am giving them to you."

"You're gonna ruin my makeup," the bride protested as her eyes welled with tears.

"You're so beautiful you don't need it," the bride's mother said, complimenting her only child.

The bride smiled at her mother and grandmother and then drew them both into her arms for a group hug.

"I love you guys so much," she said. "Now get outta here and get into the chapel so I can get married already!" They all laughed and the mother and grandmother left. Then the bride pulled her rosary from her handbag and closed her eyes. She recited the traditional Catholic prayer she'd memorized just for this occasion.

"O Jesus, lover of the young, the dearest friend I have,

in all confidence I open my heart to You to beg Your light and assistance in the important task of planning my future. Give me the light of Your grace, that I may decide wisely concerning the person who is to be my partner through life. Dearest Jesus, send me such a one whom in Your divine wisdom You judge best suited to be united with me in marriage. May his character reflect some of the traits of Your own sacred heart. May he be upright, loyal, pure, sincere, and noble, so that with united efforts and with pure and unselfish love we both may strive to perfect ourselves in soul and body, as well as the children it may please You to entrust to our care. Bless our friendship before marriage, that sin may have no part in it. May our mutual love bind us so closely that our future home may ever be most like Your own at Nazareth.

"O Mary Immaculate, sweet mother of the young, to your special care I entrust the decision I am to make as to my future husband. You are my guiding star! Direct me to the person with whom I can best cooperate in doing God's holy will, with whom I can live in peace, love, and harmony in this life and attain eternal joys in the next. Amen."

The bride opened her eyes, confident that God would answer her prayers. He always did. In fact, He already had. After all, He'd sent her the most perfect man in the world, the love of her life, her soul mate. Now they were about to be joined in holy matrimony. It was every woman's dream.

The bride could barely contain her elation at the fact that out of all the people in the world, she'd met her perfect match. Her groom-to-be was handsome, ambitious, and he adored her and treated her like a queen. He loved her for who she was on the inside, not just for her body, and she knew that was a real blessing. She was a lucky girl indeed.

The bride smoothed out her full hoopskirt made of heavy beaded silk and twirled giddily. Then taking one last look in the mirror, she pulled her crystal-encrusted veil over her face and prepared to take the biggest step of her life.

Chapter 1
THE LiFE

As THE SUN ROSE above the icy waters of Lake Michigan and sunlight began to stream through the blinds of a luxury high-rise apartment, Ricardo Diaz rolled over in the large silk-sheeted bed he occupied and grabbed a handful of his bedmate's ample bosom. He squeezed the firm golden mounds, tweaking the hardening dark nipples until the woman lying next to him stirred and moaned. Ricardo's hands began to travel down her abdomen until he reached her box and opened it. His fingers moved expertly, flicking her pleasure button until her juices began to flow. Without saying a word, Ricardo inserted his rock-hard manhood into the woman and began to thrust slowly in and out of her wet sweetness.

"Ay, Papi," the woman moaned, thrusting her hips against him in perfect harmony.

"That's right, girl," Ricardo said, encouraging his lover, pumping faster.

He fondled the woman's breasts and played with her engorged clitoris until he could feel her walls contract around his hardness and she shuddered and shivered with delight. Ricardo loved the way it felt when a woman came for him. There was nothing on earth like it, the high was incomparable, except for the high he got when he was making money. New pussy and new money were things that made life sweet for a baller like Ricardo Diaz and he had plenty of both.

Engulfed in the warm and throbbing sexy *mami* he was piping, Ricardo felt like a king. He always felt like a king when he was with *her*. She was his fly bitch, his *mami chula*, and not only was she fine but she was a freak.

"You like that?" Ricardo asked as he felt his lover climax again. "Come for me, Chula."

"Ooh, I'm coming for you, Papi," the woman squealed with pleasure.

Once he was convinced that his lover was satisfied, Ricardo went for his, grabbing a handful of the woman's hair and pounding her so hard that the sound of their skin slapping against each other echoed through the room like claps of thunder. Ricardo grunted and with a few final thrusts he climaxed deep within the woman, who sighed happily. Spent, Ricardo removed himself from the woman and rolled over onto his back, breathing heavily.

"Go fix me some breakfast, Gloria," Ricardo commanded, and his lady friend did as she was told. Minutes later, she returned with a cup of freshly squeezed orange juice and a cup of coffee.

"Will Belgian waffles be okay?" she asked.

"Yeah. Lots of butter, syrup, and powdered sugar."

"I'll fix them just the way you like them, Papi," she replied and went to prepare the meal.

Ricardo stretched lazily and propped his hands behind his head after clicking on the forty-two-inch plasma-screen television mounted on the bedroom wall. He went over all the things he had to do that day in his mind. After he left his Chula, he'd head to his business and make a few stacks, then he'd roll through the streets and check a couple of traps. Somewhere along the way he'd put in a call to his wife; maybe he'd take her out later to dinner and a show. But not before he got breakfast in bed and some head from his side lady, who'd returned to the bedroom with a tray of steaming-hot food. But the food would have to wait. As if she'd read his mind, Ricardo's *mami chula* climbed back into the bed and snuggled beneath the sheets, taking his manhood into her mouth and having a little breakfast of her own.

This is the life, Ricardo thought to himself as he received the blow job of a lifetime.

HEAVEN DIAZ ROLLED OVER in bed to find her husband's side empty. Again. It was the second time in a week that her husband hadn't made it home. Her intuition told her that he was unfaithful, but she willed herself to believe the excuses he fed her. *Ricardo loves me and he's working hard to build and maintain the wonderful life I have*, she often told herself.

She got out of bed and went down the stairs of her five-thousand-square-foot home and into the kitchen. She couldn't help but marvel at the kitchen fit for a chef with its stainless-steel appliances and copper pots. Heaven had every gadget and gizmo known to the culinary world, and prepared meals fit for royalty every night of the week, but her husband was rarely home to enjoy them. When she first got married she thought that there would be candlelight and champagne every night, but her childhood fantasy was quickly marred by reality. Ricardo was a workaholic and put in long hours on the job as the owner of an exotic car sales, rental, and driver service.

But Heaven definitely reaped the rewards of her husband's labor. The fabulous kitchen where she whipped up meals was inside a tight, custom-built crib nestled near the shores of Lake Michigan in the Hyde Park section of Chicago. There were six bedrooms, seven and a half baths, and an indoor swimming pool in the four-story manse. Ricardo had given Heaven carte blanche when meeting with the architect who designed the home. They spared no expense when deciding what fixtures the home would have, and it was even featured in the real estate sections of the major Chicago newspapers and in home and architecture magazines.

Heaven also had the wardrobe of a queen; every garment in her closet sported a designer label. She had more shoes than Carrie Bradshaw and Imelda Marcos combined, and she had more bling than a diamond mine in Sierra Leone. Heaven drove the exotic car of her choice and switched whips whenever the whim hit. Over the past year she'd pushed a Rover, a Lambo, a Ferrari, and a Maserati. And on the rare occasions she didn't feel like driving, she had a fleet of drivers at her disposal.

She had everything that any woman could want and then some. She had everything but her husband's time, but without sacrifice one can't attain one's goals, or at least that was Heaven's rationale. One day soon, her husband would have the time to spend with her that she craved, and maybe they could even start a family. But until then, she'd have to be resigned to living in the satisfying lap of luxury, even if it was a lonely position.

Aside from perpetual loneliness, Heaven suffered from another nagging problem. She had her doubts as to where all the material things her husband lavished on her came from. Her gut told her that something was amiss. She knew that her husband made a good living and worked extremely hard; in fact, she'd helped her husband attain much of the success that he had. Heaven made a million phone calls and put in countless hours of legwork helping her husband get his business off the ground and over the years the company flourished. But Heaven had her suspicions because little by little certain things weren't adding up.

For starters, there were the late nights, no-shows, and suspicious phone calls that Rico got all hours of the night when he did find his way home. He'd have brief, stilted conversations with whoever was on the other end. Heaven would ask her husband about those things, but his excuses always left her with far more questions than answers. Then there was the abundance of cash he always seemed to have. Most men never had more than a few hundred bucks on them, but Rico traveled with wads and wads of dough that made Heaven fear that he'd be the target of a robbery sooner or later. She told him that most businessmen used credit and that he should do the same and simply pay the bills on time, but Ricardo assured her that he knew what he was doing.

There was also the fact that they lived a lifestyle more suited to an athlete or some other celebrity and not a businessman; businessmen were usually far more understated. Ricardo and Heaven's assets were worth millions of dollars. And Ricardo never seemed to care about how much anything cost; he just bought what he wanted when he wanted. An entrepreneur usually had to be a bit more frugal and cost-conscious. But when Heaven suggested that they stack more money for a rainy day Rico balked. He told her that they had more money than they could ever spend in one lifetime and that the future held no financial worries, but his cavalier attitude only made Heaven worry more. She was concerned that perhaps her husband had been tempted by the lure of the streets.

Heaven was sweet but she wasn't stupid. She'd seen more than her share of hustlers and dope boys growing up in the tough Logan Square neighborhood of Chicago. And plenty of them had tried to win her affection but she wanted no part of that kind of life. She enjoyed glitz and glamour but was wise enough to know that material things could never be the measure of a man. And she believed that drugs were poison that were killing the masses and making the world a worse place while a select few profited. But Heaven knew that such temptations weren't always easy for a man to walk away from, and she shuddered at the mere thought that her husband could be involved in illegal activity and prayed that he wasn't so stupid or greedy. She'd been bold enough to confront Ricardo a time or two about her feelings, but he always had an explanation that made sense and Heaven had been raised to trust her husband. After all, if she couldn't trust him, what was the point of being married?

Heaven tried not to sweat her suspicions. After all, she was a child of God, and He would always look after her. And Heaven firmly believed that what was done in the dark would always come to light and the truth—if it was anything other than what her husband told her—would be revealed in due time.

Heaven sighed as she prepared to begin her day. *Flaws, worries, and all this is my life,* Heaven said to herself.

GLORIA CRUZ SUCKED RICARDO'S cock for what felt like an hour. Her jaw had a cramp and her mouth was becoming dry but that didn't curb her enthusiasm. She slurped and sucked loudly, moaning and groaning and looking up at Ricardo like he was the don of all dons. She flickered her tongue over the head of his penis and blew lightly over it before deep throating the length. Ricardo grabbed her by the hair and grunted before spurting inside of her mouth, and Gloria hungrily devoured every drop.

"I love you, Papi," she said, looking up at him with a smile on her face and sincerity in her eyes.

Gloria was crazy for Ricardo, she always had been. They'd dated off and on from the time they were twelve. She'd gone to college and they maintained their relationship until Gloria got a fellowship to study dance in Paris that she couldn't pass up. Dancing was her passion and she had the opportunity of a lifetime to follow her dream. They promised to stay together but the distance made things difficult and then Ricardo met Heaven. He'd fallen head over heels and within the space of six months they were married.

Ricardo had claimed it was an impulse, that he'd missed Gloria so much that he tried to duplicate their relationship with someone else. He claimed it was Gloria who was the love of his life, and that marrying Heaven had been a big mistake. The fact that Ricardo had moved on so quickly broke her heart and she vowed never to speak to him again, but when she returned stateside four years later they ran into each other at a party and reignited their old flame. Gloria had never stopped loving Ricardo, and she wouldn't let him go again, even if it meant that she had to share him.

The way she saw it, Ricardo was her man, and Heaven was just on borrowed time.

"I love you, too, baby," Ricardo told her, and it was the truth. He did love Gloria. He'd always loved Gloria. He just loved his wife more. When he met Heaven he knew that she was something special. Heaven was breathtakingly beautiful. Her golden skin, sparkling dark eyes, and thick luxurious hair had him enraptured immediately, and when he got to know her he knew that she would be the perfect wife.

Heaven was virginal and sweet and never gave him any problems. His relationship with Gloria had thrived on drama, heat, and intensity. Heaven trusted him blindly and was devoted and true. Gloria had been suspicious and accused him of cheating all the time. Heaven helped him with his business when it was first starting out and Ricardo knew that she would lay down her life for him. Gloria was just as committed to handling her business as he was, and Ricardo loved her hustle. But he didn't want to marry a hustler. His wife had to be all about him 24/7/365 and he had that in Heaven.

"Baby, why can't we be together?" Gloria asked him.

"We've been over this a million times. I'm married to Heaven. She's a good woman, she doesn't deserve me walking out on her."

"If she's such a good woman, why are you with me half the week?" Gloria asked him. "And do you think that I deserve to play second fiddle to her?"

"You're not second fiddle. You're a good woman, too, and I care about you and want to be with you. But you know and I know that I need a woman who is all about me. I need my wife to take care of my needs."

"I do take care of your needs," Gloria snapped. She resented it when Ricardo acted as if Heaven did something for him that she didn't.

"I need my wife to put me before herself," Ricardo said. Gloria stayed silent. "That's what I thought," he told her. "Besides, Heaven is more Catholic than the pope. She'd never give me a divorce. Now, Chula, let's not talk about this, okay? I love you, and that's all that matters. I have to go to work." Ricardo got up to take a shower while Gloria flopped on the bed, crossed her arms in front of her chest, and pouted. Ricardo reached into the pocket of the pants he'd been wearing the night before and pulled out a bankroll.

"I've got something that will make you feel better," Ricardo told Gloria, tossing her the wad of cash that was bound by a thick green rubber band. "I've got to roll down to Miami to pick up a car for my personal collection. I want you to come with me. So go buy yourself some fly shit. I want you to be the sexiest bitch on the beach. If you need more, hit me on the hip and I got you."

Gloria grinned, thumbing through the stack of bills. There was a couple thousand dollars there. She'd definitely need more, but this was a good start. Ricardo went to take his shower and Gloria went to clean the kitchen. Suddenly, a wave of nausea hit her like a tsunami, causing her to run to the second bathroom of her penthouse apartment and heave into the toilet. Gloria emptied the contents of her stomach into the bowl and then flushed. She rinsed her mouth out with some water and mouthwash and then stared at her reflection in the mirror.

Gloria smiled when she realized that her period was a couple of days late. She knew in her gut that she was pregnant. Now she had the perfect ammunition against her nemesis Heaven, and it was growing inside of her. Ricardo would never turn his back on his child. Never. And Gloria was hoping that Heaven was the type of woman who would put up with a lot of shit, but not an outside child. That would be grounds for her to get an annulment. Then she and Ricardo could be together forever, the way it was intended.

It's going to be the life, Gloria mused.

Chapter 2
OWNER OF A LONELY HEART

A GROUP OF ROWDY seventh- and eighth-graders chattered and chased one another around a classroom but instantly settled down when Heaven entered.

"Good morning, kids," Heaven said enthusiastically. Heaven taught art at the Latin American Association twice a week. She loved working with the children; it gave her life a sense of meaning. And the thrill she got when she was able to open a child up and express his or her creative side was incomparable to anything.

"Good morning, Miss Heaven," the children sang in unison.

"Please take out your collages," Heaven instructed, then walked around the room inspecting them all, doling out compliments and words of encouragement. Each child smiled and beamed with pride, happy that their pretty and sweet teacher was pleased with their efforts.

"Where's your collage, sweetie?" Heaven asked a young girl named Consuela. Although Heaven tried to treat all the children equally, she held a special fondness for Consuela. She reminded Heaven so much of herself at that age and she had an amazing artistic gift. Consuela had unlimited potential and Heaven loved the fact that she was playing an instrumental part in helping to tap into that potential.

"I'm sorry, Miss Heaven," she said sadly. "I don't have my assignment."

"Well, that's not like you. Is everything okay?" Heaven asked with concern.

"Her daddy got locked up!" A student named Ritchie pointed at Consuela and laughed, taunting her.

"At least I know my daddy," Consuela retorted.

"Okay, kids, that's enough," Heaven scolded. "Consuela, I'll talk to you after," she said, thinking it was best to let the issue ride until the end of the class. If what Ritchie said was true, Heaven didn't want Consuela to feel any worse than she already had to be feeling.

When the class was over, Heaven ushered the other children out and closed the door behind them.

"Now, tell me what's going on, Consuela. Is what Ritchie said true? Did your father get locked up?"

"Yeah," Consuela said sadly, looking at her feet. "He was on parole from a stupid mistake he made a while ago. He got fired from his job. The marshals came and took him away a couple of days ago; they said he was in violation. It's messed up because he was really trying to get his act together."

"Why did he get fired?" Heaven probed.

"The person he worked for was taking money out of his check for all kinds of things that my father felt was unfair. His boss knew that most of the people who were working for him really needed their jobs and couldn't do anything about the way they got treated. My dad got sick of it and stood up for himself. He got fired."

"That sucks," Heaven said empathetically.

"Yeah," Consuela said. "He worked at a car wash. He didn't even make minimum wage because they got tips. The owner made him pay for getting his uniform cleaned even though my mom washed it. That man even charged my father and his other workers for cleaning supplies."

"Not only is that unfair," Heaven said, furrowing her brow in anger, "it's illegal!"

"What can we do about it?" Consuela asked. "We're poor, and my father has a record."

"Let me worry about that," Heaven said, pulling out her cell phone and placing a phone call.

"Rico, it's me. I need your help," she told her husband when he answered his cell phone. Heaven wanted to question Rico about where he'd been all night but refrained. This issue with Consuela was much more important.

"What's wrong?" Rico asked. "Are you okay?"

"I'm fine, but it's one of my students. Her father's in a bind." Heaven explained the situation to Rico.

"You're such a bleeding heart, Heaven," Rico said. "I swear that if you could you'd help any and every person with a sob story."

"Probably," Heaven replied. "But do you think that we can do something about *this* one?"

"Yeah, babe, sure. If it means that much to you, I'll put a lawyer on the case and hire the girl's father here at the dealership. I can always use good help detailing the fleet and stuff."

"Thanks, Rico," Heaven said and gave him the information about where Consuela's father was being held.

"I love you, Heaven," Rico told his wife. "You're a beautiful person inside and out, you know that?"

"Thanks, honey. I love you, too," Heaven said.

"I mean it, Heaven. You've got a good heart," Rico replied.

"Well, I try," Heaven said with a giggle.

"I'll be home early tonight," Rico promised. "I know I've been putting in a lot of hours at the office but tonight I want to spend some quality time with my wonderful wife."

"I can't wait," Heaven told him.

Heaven disconnected the call and smiled warmly at Consuela. "Don't worry, sweetie. My husband's got a lawyer on the case and he's going to give your dad a job. He'll be home soon, you'll see."

"My family can't afford a lawyer," Consuela said.

"No one asked your family to pay," Heaven told her with a wink.

Consuela's eyes filled with tears. "Why?" she asked. "Why are you doing this for me?"

"You're a good girl, Consuela, and you're lucky to have a father who's sticking around and trying to provide for your family. Everyone stumbles from time to time, and if I can give a hand up, I do."

"Still . . . you're not even my real teacher or anything. This isn't school, it's an after-school program."

"It doesn't matter to me, Consuela. You're a special girl, don't ever forget that. You can do whatever you want to if you put your mind to it, work hard, and keep God first in your life. Promise me you'll do those things, and I'll look out for you as much as I can."

Without warning Consuela threw her arms around Heaven and squeezed her tight.

"Thank you so much, Miss Heaven. Thank you!"

"You're welcome, Consuela," Heaven said, squeezing her back.

"I love you, Miss Heaven. You're like an angel."

Heaven was so choked up she couldn't even respond. She just held her student and prayed that God would bless Consuela and her family.

AFTER HEAVEN FINISHED UP at her art class, she stopped at the grocery store to pick up a few things before heading home. She was so pleased with her husband for helping one of her students that she wanted to prepare a special dinner for him. She purchased thick steaks, a bottle of red wine, and flowers and candles with which to decorate the dinner table. She also bought ingredients to make a key lime pie: Rico's favorite.

Upon her return to their home, Heaven immediately went to work. She pulled her hair up into a bun on top of her head, changed into a sweatsuit, and then went to work making the key lime pie, seasoning and marinating the steak, and preparing *mofongo*, a Puerto Rican dish made of plantains and pork cracklings that was another one of

Rico's favorites. When Rico arrived, Heaven planned on throwing the steaks on the grill while they sipped wine and talked, and then they'd have a nice romantic dinner topped off with dessert in bed. Heaven thrilled at the thought of making love to her husband and rushed upstairs to take a shower and slip into something sexy.

Hours went by and there was no word from Rico. She called his office and his cell and sent him a couple of text messages, but he didn't reply until it was nearly midnight.

"I'm sorry but I'm going to be really late," Rico explained. "Don't wait up," he said and hung up without even waiting for her response.

Heaven fumed. She went into the kitchen and grabbed the steaks and shoved them down the garbage disposal, followed by the *mofongo*. Then she opened the bottle of wine and took a swig directly from the bottle before devouring the key lime pie all by herself within minutes. She finished off the bottle of wine soon thereafter before staggering up the stairs and passing out across her bed.

RICO FELT A TWINGE of guilt as Gloria rode his dick like an experienced rodeo cowgirl. He'd promised Heaven that he would be home early and he'd had every intention on keeping that promise, but then Gloria called him and asked him to swing through after he left the dealership. At first he told her no; he didn't want to disappoint his wife. But then Gloria started in with the freaky phone talk and he couldn't resist as her words provoked a rock-hard erection. Gloria had the magnetic pull of a tractor beam; Rico could rarely resist her no matter how hard he tried. He'd only planned on staying about an hour, long enough to have a drink and get a quick blow job, but the blow job led to them ravaging each other like animals in the sack.

Almost as if she were a psychic, Gloria seemed to sense that Rico's mind was elsewhere.

"Look at me!" she commanded. "I don't want your mind or your eyes anywhere else but on me." Gloria increased the speed at which she ground her hips against Rico's and held his head in place so that she was staring him directly in the eyes.

"You like that, don't you, baby?" Gloria purred.

"Yes," Rico groaned.

"Tell me you love me!" Gloria ordered. Rico didn't answer. He just let out a shout as he climaxed, but that didn't deter Gloria. She held him inside her walls and fondled his scrotum. Rico squirmed beneath her before pushing her off him.

"You trippin', girl," Rico said, shaking his head.

"Say it, Rico! Tell me you love me!" Gloria screamed.

Rico looked at her like she'd lost her mind but Gloria didn't back down. She just crossed her arms and waited for Rico's declaration.

"I love you, Gloria, okay?" Rico finally replied. "Damn!"

"Then why wouldn't you say it? Why did the cat have your tongue?" Gloria interrogated.

"Chill, Glory," Rico said, getting up to take a shower.

"You're not leaving, are you?" Gloria asked.

"I've got to get home. I already flaked out on Heaven," Rico explained.

"I don't give a fuck about that bitch!" Gloria spat.

"Watch your mouth," Rico warned. "Heaven is my wife and I won't allow you to disrespect her."

Before Gloria could protest, Rico stormed into the bathroom. He turned on the water and hopped in the shower. He quickly soaped his muscular, caramel-colored body under the cool spray and rinsed off. As he dipped his head under the stream of water, he heard Gloria banging on the bathroom door. Rico had the foresight to lock it behind him; he knew how temperamental Gloria was and didn't want her barging in and picking a fight. He just wanted to get home to his wife.

"Open this fucking door!" Gloria shouted. Rico didn't respond. He finished his shower and turned the water off.

Rico emerged from the bathroom with a towel wrapped around his waist. He made a beeline past her and went straight for his clothes, which were crumpled in a heap on the floor. Normally he would have asked Gloria to knock the wrinkles out with an iron, but he knew not to test her when she was in such a feisty mood. He pulled his clothes on and searched for his shoes.

"You know, I'm getting tired of this, Rico," Gloria complained.

"That makes two of us," he told her.

"What's that supposed to mean?" Gloria asked.

"It means that if you stress me every single time that I come over here, I'm going to eventually stop coming here. Is that what you want?" Rico asked.

"No," Gloria replied. "I just want us to be together."

"When we're together, we're together. And when we aren't, we aren't. That's just how it is," Rico told Gloria, and left.

HEAVEN'S EYELIDS FLUTTERED OPEN the minute she felt her husband get in the bed. She wanted so badly to ask him where he'd been, but didn't. Her mouth felt dry, her head was throbbing from the wine, and she couldn't think straight. She was in no condition to talk about anything with Rico, and within minutes she was back asleep. She was plagued with nightmares and she tossed and turned fretfully until the sun shone in through the drapes. When she awoke, she rolled over to find that Rico was gone, but what else was new and what could she do about it?

Heaven Diaz was raised to be a good Catholic girl. She was named Heaven because her parents had believed her to be a gift from God the minute they'd laid eyes on their angelic baby girl. Her *abuela* taught her that if she followed the word of God that everything in her life would fall into place and so far that had been the case. She'd attended mass faithfully as well as confession and read the Bible daily, and she not only prayed but had faith in her prayers. As a result she had a beautiful home, the comfort of living in luxury, and a husband who loved her, even if he wasn't around much. She felt bad for complaining.

Still, deep inside, like most good girls, Heaven occasionally longed to be bad. Heaven wanted to confront her husband about his nights out. She wanted to question him at length about where his money came from. She wanted to demand that he stop sleeping with other women and do the nasty things he did with them with her and her alone. She wanted to be a freak in bed, maybe even cheat on him and give him a taste of his own medicine. But she knew that those things would never be accepted and so she didn't do them. Instead, the frustration and resentment of being loved yet neglected began to build and fester within her. She couldn't help but be angry with Ricardo. He ignored her, left her alone, paid little attention to her, and took her for granted. And yet she still loved him.

Ricardo was Heaven's first boyfriend, her first love, her first lover, her first everything. Before she met him her life had been about church and school and her favorite pastime, drawing. She'd spend hours alone reading and designing clothes or listening to music, and she'd always lived at home with her parents and grandmother even though she was an adult. She had no desire to live life in the fast lane . . . until she met Ricardo.

They met at the Puerto Rican Day Parade in Logan Square five years before. Ricardo was loaning his convertible Corvette and a classic Cutlass to a friend who was participating and Heaven was marching with the kids from the Latin American Association. It was love at first sight for both of them. Ricardo opened up a new world to Heaven, full of designer clothes and beautiful jewelry and exotic trips. He treated her like a princess and always gave her the utmost respect. Heaven had every reason in the world to be happy, but she wasn't. Her heart was filled with pain and she longed for something, anything, to make it go away.

Chapter 3
THE REAL

RICARDO ROLLED HIS MERCEDES SL65 AMG down Michigan Avenue until he reached his auto dealership. He always got a high when he saw the fleet of gleaming exotic cars and limos in the lot, and the tall lighted sign that read DIAZ BROTHERS IMPORT AUTO. At twenty-nine years of age, Panamanian-born Ricardo Diaz was at the top of his game. He'd come a long way from his childhood days in the tough Englewood neighborhood where he grew up on Chicago's South Side. Being black and Latino and poor, the Diazes had to overcome all kinds of trials and tribulations. Back then, he and his family didn't have a pot to piss in or a window to throw it out. Now he had windows in cribs all over the world.

Ricardo's father cut out on his mother and younger

brother when they were toddlers, and she struggled to make a good living for her boys. Ricardo's mother found work at a local McDonald's thanks to the owner, Francisco Perez, a black Panamanian immigrant himself who was one of Chicago's most successful businessmen. A hero in both the black and Latino communities, Perez mentored many young men and women who wanted a way out of the ghetto and Ricardo's mother was one of them. With Mr. Perez's help, she worked her way up to manager and eventually became the owner of two franchises herself. Ricardo and his brother learned the value of hard work from their mother's example, but they had no desire to become hamburger kings. They had bigger dreams and bigger dollar signs in mind.

Ricardo pulled the Benz into his parking space and headed inside.

"Good morning, Mr. Diaz." His secretary, Keisha, greeted him with a smile.

"Good morning, Keisha," Ricardo said, flashing his dimpled megawatt smile.

Ricardo had hit it a couple of times, then passed her off to one of his boys, but there was still chemistry between them and they flirted with each other constantly. Keisha was a real stunner, a petite cutie with big boobs and a penchant for rough sex. Ricardo couldn't help but smile when he thought about how he'd pounded her on top of his desk and that's why he kept her around. Friendly eye candy was definitely a plus in his business and he was training her to become a salesperson because he knew she'd be able to pull in a lot of bodies.

"Your wife called," Keisha told Ricardo.

"Yup," Ricardo said, nonchalantly walking into his office and shutting the door. Ricardo pulled out his cell and punched in a number.

"What's the haps with them traps?" he asked his business partner and brother, Joaquin. Ricardo was referring to their other enterprise, moving bricks of coca through the Chi-town streets. On the outside, the Diaz brothers appeared to be hardworking, law-abiding citizens who had used their smarts and connections to build an empire. They'd been featured in some local papers and magazines as entrepreneurs to watch, but there was a part of their enterprise that they didn't want anyone watching, and that was their dope hustle. But being watched by the feds wasn't a problem. Theirs was a multilevel organization that was cloaked in secrecy.

Neither Joaquin nor Ricardo were visible players in the game. They had another partner for that and he was excellent at rallying street troops with fierce loyalty. Besides, they had the local authorities in their pocket, as well as a few important people in Chicago politics. Plenty of policemen, aldermen, city councilmen, and state and county workers owed the Diaz brothers favors.

"Everything is running smoothly. The shipments have been distributed and the money's been collected. I'll be bringing you the paperwork tonight. And the meeting is set up for Miami," Joaquin told him.

"Good to hear, Kino," Ricardo replied, using his childhood nickname for his younger brother.

"Yeah, but I got a little news that isn't so good. Those dudes from across the bridge been talking mad shit. Word on the streets is they're planning a takeover."

"That'll never happen," Ricardo said coolly. "Never."

"True dat, but just in case I think I'm gonna talk to the big man. Make sure we got all our bases covered."

"I'm gonna cut outta here in a little bit. I'll go talk to the big man myself," Ricardo said.

"You sure?" Kino asked. "I've got the time."

"I'm sure," Ricardo told him. He knew his brother was hot-blooded and could escalate a delicate situation quickly.

"Cool. Why don't we let the wives get together tonight so we can discuss our business face-to-face without them interrupting? We can take them to dinner and then we'll go back to your spot and they can talk while we work on a few things," Kino suggested.

"Sounds like just what I had in mind, but let's make it tomorrow."

"Why not tonight?" Kino asked.

"Man, I've been fucking up with the wifey in a major way. I need to spend some quality time with her and defuse the situation before it blows up in my face."

"I feel you, bro. Take care of home. You wanna link up tomorrow around seven?"

"That'll work. I'll see you then."

Ricardo spent a couple hours at the dealership and then hit the streets. His first stop was to roll by the Ickes Homes, one of the few remaining housing projects in the city of Chicago. The mayor had all but destroyed the projects and had erected pricey new townhomes and condos in their place. All eyes were on Ricardo and his $200,000 whip as he rolled through the development at a slow crawl. Most people drove through the Ickes as fast as they could, but not Ricardo. He had the Ickes on lock and no one was going to dare fuck with him. He pulled in front of the building he was going to visit and got out. A tall and lanky teenage boy named Rah came over to the car.

"What up, Rico," he said.

"You know the business, Rah," Rico said. "Politics as usual. Is big man upstairs?"

"Yeah, man, but you don't want to go up there. The elevator is broken. I'll go get him," Rah offered.

"Good looking," Rico told Rah.

Within minutes, a seven-foot-tall, handsome black man with a stocky build came out of the building.

"Hyckef, big man, what's going on?" Rico asked him, giving him a pound.

"It's all good, chief. Let's take a ride, man."

The two men got into Rico's car and rolled through the streets of the South Side, discussing the business they had at hand.

"What's this I hear about some beef with the G.I. Boys?" Ricardo asked Hyckef, referring to a cartel of coke pushers in Gary, Indiana. For years, the two clans had been able to transact business with no static or friction, but the concrete jungle was abuzz with words like "takeover" and "setups." Rico didn't like it.

"These dudes is just mad they not getting cake the way we are. They tried to open a rim shop over there with a recording studio in it, but that shit flopped. I heard their setup was tight but there just wasn't enough ballers in G.I. to keep they shit afloat. Them motherfuckers is just jealous and letting off a little steam, flapping they jaws. But they don't want to go to war with us. Our army is ready for anything."

"Yeah, I hear you, but I'm not really trying to go to war. I ain't no punk but I like my life quiet. These motherfuckers might feel they got to make a move to prove a point."

"And then I'll have to make a move to prove my point, and my point is hollow point. I'm telling you, this shit is no problem. Them Gary boys is not about to come over here to the Chi and start a damn thing. And if they start some shit, I'll finish the shit."

"I know you will," Ricardo told him. "Let's just not let it get that far. I got a legit business I gotta take care of and build, too. We're starting to steal some of the business from those dealerships on the Gold Coast, and I know it's just a matter of time before we can quit this shit for good."

"Why would you want to quit, man?" Hyckef asked him. "The money is good."

"But the life isn't. Man, we both know that these streets don't really love us. That's the real."

"Man, either you trap or you die," Hyckef argued. "*That's* the real."

"Yeah, but you got to constantly elevate your game. What we do now has some risk even though our shit's tight. When we finish setting up the legit shit the way we want it, we'll have no risk. At least not the same kinds of risks. Won't be no jail time or wars popping off."

"Ain't gon' be no jail time or war no way. We own this

fucking city," Hyckef boasted cockily. It was an argument the two of them had had several times before. Hyckef was a lifer, he wanted to stay married to the streets until death did them part. Although he had a tight condo with lakefront and skyline views, he preferred to spend his time in the 'jects with his hood rat of the moment. But Rico had bigger and better things, legit things in mind. He was working his plan and only had a little way to go until he was out of the game for good, but Hyckef felt as long as there was money in the streets he'd be there, too.

Hyckef and Ricardo had been friends since they were in the ninth grade and had always had each other's back. If Ricardo had a problem, Hyckef was there to handle it. And if Hyckef had talked himself into a crazy situation, Ricardo was there to smooth talk his way out of it. Ricardo's mouthpiece and smarts and Hyckef's size and fearless nature made one hell of a combination. And Joaquin and Ricardo's Panamanian heritage made finding a connect very easy. All it took was one fateful trip to Miami to visit their cousin, and they had a couple keys on consignment and built from there. Rico had no intentions of destroying the empire they'd all worked so hard to build.

"Hyckef, you're like a brother to me, you know that. Without you, this organization would be nothing. It's taken years of hard work to get to where we are, and now it's all paying off," Rico told his friend.

"So what's your point? You trust me to handle this, right?" Hyckef asked with bloodlust in his eyes.

"It's not that I don't trust you. I'm just concerned that your hot head and itchy trigger finger will eventually lead to our downfall."

Chapter 4
BLACK-HEARTED

April 2007, Gary, Indiana

BLACK, THE LEADER OF the G.I. Boys, was covered by the darkness of night as he cut the headlights on his black Ford Taurus and parked a few doors down from an abandoned house on a near-deserted street in Gary. After the descent of the steel industry, the once-thriving town had seen better days and now had a reputation as one of the most hard-core cities in the Midwest, but there were changes being made and Black knew that his criminal organization had to change with them. The newly elected mayor, Rudy Clay, had increased police presence and was taking a hard stance on illegal activity, especially interstate activity between Illinois and Indiana. Running drugs and guns was getting harder—harder, but not impossible.

The year before there had been a sweep in the Steel City so devastating that it nearly wiped his crew, the G.I. Boys, out. No drugs, at least nothing of any major weight, were coming in because all the major players had been knocked, and their connects in neighboring Hammond, Indiana, and the suburbs of Chicago didn't want to fuck with them for fear of having an unwanted light shone on them. But Black had plenty of family and friends on the Chi's South Side, a mere thirty minutes away, and he made sure he used them. His elderly aunts and uncles, his young nieces and nephews, and his cousins were all part of the business, and they transported whatever needed to be moved using a variety of methods. And Black paid off every crooked cop there was to pay off.

Because of Black's creativity and loyal family, it wasn't hard for him to rise to the top of the dope game in Gary. But no matter how many pockets he greased and no matter how many new players and clever plays he added to the mix, he knew he couldn't rest easy. Black's ascent in the game came with a price. It's lonely at the top. You have to do things to stay there that you never thought you'd have to do. Black had bodied so many cats that he'd grown up with he thought that their ghosts would haunt his conscience forever, but what choice did he have? The rules of the game were finite and simple: Kill or be killed.

Black knew he had to make a move out of G.I. to Chicago, where there was more money and he would war with enemies and not childhood friends. If he had to have blood on his hands, it may as well belong to someone he didn't give a fuck about. So Black devised a strategy, one that would help him define the territory he was soon to take over. He wasn't about to walk across enemy lines without a plan.

Black had his peeps in Chicago on reconnaissance for months, watching and analyzing every aspect of the dope game in the Chi. They watched hustlers on the South Side, the West Side, and the North Side. They studied every type of drug gang there was from a distance: the blacks, the whites, the Latinos, the Russians, and the Serbians. Then the troops moved in closer. Black sent in moles to infiltrate gangs, paid commissary for people in jail to get info from known snitches, and he even put sexy women on the payroll to gather information from the local dopeboys by seducing them. When it was all said and done, he knew precisely the territory he wanted to take over, that belonging to the Diaz brothers.

Hardly anyone knew that the Diaz brothers were behind a drug empire, but hardly anyone put as much work into their hustle as Black. Other hustlers were greedy and shortsighted; they didn't see the big picture. They either moved too swiftly, governed by their emotions, or they took what they saw and heard at face value like a gossiping girl. Black was too smart to get caught out there like a sucker. He took his work very, very seriously. That was the only way he was going to get ahead. Black had the insight to know that for every face that was visible in the dope game, there were plenty who were behind the scenes directing the play. Black simply didn't stop looking until he knew who controlled what, from Chicago all the way to Colombia, Panama, and Peru.

Black pulled two burners from under the passenger's seat. He checked the ammo and put the guns in his pockets. He regretted having to do what he was about to do, but it was inevitable. Earlier Black learned that one of his top sergeants, Bishop, had been feeding information to the enemy, a stickup kid turned hustler named Rock who was trying to make a name for himself. Bishop and Rock were planning to murk Black and take over his business, but luckily Black's cousin Sharnette heard the two dudes planning the whole thing out at the barbershop where she cut hair.

The betrayal burned Black not just because he'd been good to Bishop, putting him on when he didn't have a pot

to piss in and was fresh out the joint, but because they'd dis-
cussed killing him out in the open like he was some kind
of bitch not to be feared. They'd even been foolish enough
to discuss the fact that they'd scored five bricks of cocaine
and were splitting the product in the basement of the abandoned house. Not only were the knuckleheads disloyal and
bold with it, they were sloppy as fuck. There was no way
that Black could let either of them live.

Black pulled his hoodie over his head and got out of the
car. He'd considered wearing a ski mask just in case some
nosy neighbor was looking out of her window, but decided
against it. He wanted the motherfucking traitors to see his
face when he ended their miserable lives. Black walked as
silently and stealthily as a panther around to the back of
the house. He took a deep breath and kicked in the back
door.

Bishop and Rock were amateurs. They didn't have the
sense or foresight to put a soldier at the door so he had a
clear path to the basement. Neither Bishop nor Rock had
a chance to reach for their weapons. Black drew down and
let off two shots. A bullet seared into the chest of each of
his adversaries, throwing the bodies violently out of their
chairs. Bishop and Rock lay on the floor gasping for air as
their punctured lungs filled with blood. Black walked over
to Bishop and stood over him.

"How could you shit on me, man?" Black asked. Fear

was in Bishop's eyes as he clutched his chest and struggled to breathe. "We were friends. I've known your ass forever. And you cross me like this? This death is too good for you," Black said coldly as he pulled the trigger once more, landing a bullet in Bishop's dome. He would have let the bastard bleed to death in that basement, but he knew better than to leave a potential witness, especially one who'd already shown he was a traitor.

Black turned to Rock and sneered. He squeezed the trigger without saying a word. Then he took the bricks of product that were on the table, shoved them inside his hoodie, and left the house as quickly as he entered.

Chapter 5
THESE ARE MY CONFESSIONS

RICO HELD HIS HANDS behind his back as he entered his home. Heaven was sitting on the living room sofa with her sketch pad.

"Hey, baby," Rico said softly. He smiled at Heaven, testing the waters between them. Heaven looked up from her drawing momentarily and glowered at Rico before returning to her artwork.

"Whatcha drawing?" he asked.

"Does it matter?" Heaven asked.

"Of course it does," Rico said.

"Does it, Rico? Do you actually care what I do?" Heaven slammed her drawing pad and charcoals on the table.

"Of course I care what you do. What kind of question is that?" Rico asked.

"What, you don't understand it? Here, let me rephrase the question then. Where were you last night?" Heaven's voice rose an octave and her breathing was heavy.

"I'm sorry, baby. I got tied up at work and it couldn't be avoided," Rico explained.

Heaven shook her head. "Yeah, right," she said sarcastically.

"It's the truth," Rico said.

"Please," Heaven said, waving her hand at him.

"I know you're mad at me. I don't blame you," Rico told her. "When I came home, I could tell that you'd made a special dinner for me. I feel terrible about not keeping my promise." He whipped a huge bouquet of exotic flowers from behind his back. "These are for you."

"Gee, thanks, flowers," Heaven said flatly, not bothering to hide her disappointment.

"I got you something else, too," Rico said. He pulled a velvet box from his pocket and handed it to Heaven. Heaven took the box and put it on the table without opening it.

"Don't be that way," Rico said softly. "Open it."

Heaven continued to pout. Rico picked up the box and opened it for her. He held it in front of her face and Heaven couldn't look away. She was mesmerized at the platinum band embellished with sparkling channel-set pink diamonds.

"It's beautiful," Heaven said.

"Like you. I want you to wear this with your engagement ring and wedding band," Rico said, slipping the ring on her left hand. "It symbolizes that marrying you is the best thing I've ever done, and I'd do it again and again. I love you so much," Rico told his wife.

"Really?" Heaven asked. "You aren't getting tired of me or bored with me?"

"How can you say that?" Rico asked.

"Because you're never around. There's got to be a reason. You probably want to leave me but don't know how."

"Don't be crazy! There's a reason I'm not around much and it's because I love you and I want to give you the world. I know sometimes I get consumed with my work, but it's all for you. I'd never leave you."

"You promise?" Heaven asked.

"I promise."

Rico leaned in and kissed his wife passionately. All the anger she had instantly melted. Rico gently peeled his wife's clothes from her body and kissed her all over. Heaven was writhing and moaning, and her ecstasy was reaching a fever pitch.

"Let's go upstairs," Heaven suggested breathlessly.

"No," Rico said. "I want you right here, right now."

Swiftly, Rico entered her and stroked her deeply and

slowly. He told her he loved her over and over again, stroked her hair, and kissed her. When Heaven climaxed, tears of joy ran down her face.

"I'm sorry that I doubted you," Heaven said as she and Rico lay together in postcoital bliss.

"I'm not perfect, Heaven. I'm a man. But I'm a man who loves you, never forget that. We're going to be together until death do us part," Rico told her, and he meant every word.

IN THE MORNING, HEAVEN served her husband breakfast in bed and they made love again. By the time she kissed him good-bye at the door it was nearly noon.

"I want you to go shopping and pick up something sexy," Rico told Heaven as he left. "Tonight we're going out to dinner with Kino and Ysette."

Heaven agreed happily. She loved spending time with her brother- and sister-in-law. They were so much fun and the four of them always had a blast together. Heaven went upstairs and took a quick shower, got dressed, and typed her to-do list into her PDA. Then she went to the garage. She contemplated taking the Rover parked there, but decided against it. Her husband's chocolate brown Jaguar convertible was a much better choice on such a nice spring day.

When Heaven got in the car she looked on the backseat to find a pile of clothes that Rico needed to take to the cleaners. She ran back into the house and grabbed a plastic shopping bag to put them in and then popped the trunk to put the bag inside. There were two large cardboard boxes in the trunk. Heaven attempted to lift one but it was very heavy.

"What is this man toting around in the trunk?" Heaven muttered and then peered inside one of the boxes. She gasped and took a couple steps back when she caught sight of the contents. There was a large digital scale, plastic wrap, Vaseline, and a money counter inside.

"I know this isn't what I think it is," Heaven said out loud.

She inspected the contents more carefully. There was a chalky white residue on the scale's tray. Heaven ran her fingers over the tray and then lifted them to her mouth. She didn't know exactly what she was supposed to taste, but she saw the cops do it on television whenever they came across what they thought was drugs. She figured if it was safe for an officer of the law to do, it was probably safe for her. Her heart thumped wildly as she poked out her tongue and ran it across her fingers. The substance tasted bitter and she knew it had to be cocaine or, worse, heroin. Heaven's body shook as she slammed the trunk shut. She knew exactly where she needed to go and exactly what she needed to do.

"IN THE NAME OF the Father and of the Son and of the Holy Spirit." Heaven made the sign of the cross. "It's been three days since my last confession. Forgive me, Father, for I have sinned," Heaven told the priest on the other side of the confessional at St. Monica Church.

"Go ahead, my child," he replied.

"Father, I'm so confused I don't know what to do. In the past I've suspected my husband of adultery, and it made me so angry. But he always had an explanation for his behavior. Still, in my heart, I *knew* that he was cheating so the anger never really went away. I've tried to fight the feelings but it's so hard. Sometimes I want something bad to happen to him. I want him to hurt the way that I do. That's wrong, isn't it, Father?"

"It isn't good to wish ill things on others. You're having a natural human reaction to your fears, but I encourage you to lean heavier on your faith now. Fortify yourself with God's word and pray for a healing in your marriage," the priest said.

"I will, Father. And I've been trying. But there's something else."

"What is it, child?"

"My husband is involved in illegal activities. I've been turning a blind eye for years even though I know it's so wrong, but I can't do it anymore. I found drug paraphernalia in his car. He may have brought that poison into our home," Heaven said.

"Is your husband a Christian?" the priest asked.

"Sure he is, but I don't see what that has to do with anything."

"I ask because it is a wife's duty to pray for her husband when he is lost. A wife's prayers can lead her husband back to the Church."

"Look, my knees are just about worn-out from praying for my husband. And I've invited him to mass until I turned blue in the face. I *know* that nothing can change without Jesus' help, but I'm beginning to feel like Jesus isn't hearing my prayers because nothing seems to be happening." Heaven started to sob softly out of frustration.

"You must have patience. All of His works are according to His perfect plan. God hears your prayers. But you must eventually make a decision if you are going to live with your husband in darkness or make some tough decisions," the priest told her.

"Divorce is not an option," Heaven quickly stated.

"I wasn't going to suggest it. But if your life is in danger or your safety is threatened, an annulment would be in order."

"I don't want an annulment either, but I certainly don't want to be married to a cheating drug dealer. I want my husband at home with me where he belongs, not in the streets doing who knows what and certainly not in another woman's bed," Heaven said angrily. She sighed and ran her hands through her hair. "I'm sorry, Father. See what this is doing to me?"

"You are under a lot of pressure. I want you to pray your rosary and ask for patience, forgiveness, and discernment."

"I will, Father," Heaven said.

The priest gave Heaven some words of absolution and concluded the confession. Heaven could see him make the sign of the cross through the vents in the confessional and made it along with him. "Give thanks to the Lord for He is good," the priest said.

"For His mercy endures forever," Heaven said, and left the confessional.

AT LEAST TWICE A week Heaven went to confession. Her *abuela* had raised her to believe that confession was good for the soul; it was a dangerous thing to let evil thoughts linger within the head and heart without seeking spiritual guidance, but today Heaven left the confessional more confused than she'd ever been. She needed real, concrete answers; she needed to know exactly what to do. She could confront her husband and tell him what she'd found and demand an explanation; she could refuse to back down until he told her the truth. But what *was* the truth? How could she believe anything that Rico said?

Heaven wished that she had someone else to confide in other than a priest. She'd never had many friends, preferring to keep her inner circle small, and the few friends she did have were all busy with their work and their own families. She didn't want to be a downer and she already knew what her girls would say. They'd tell her that she had nothing to complain or worry about, and they'd tell her how lucky she was. They'd tell her that all men were dogs and to get over it, because at least she didn't have to worry about paying bills and making ends meet like they did.

Heaven looked at the beautiful ring that Rico had given her the night before. Her heart softened a little. She *knew* her husband loved her, he was just very misguided. Heaven decided to pretend she hadn't seen anything and to do what the priest said, but with a twist. She had to rely on her faith now more than ever *and* she had to fight fire with fire. She was going to go head-to-head with the competition—whether it was a woman or the streets—and she was going to come out on top, because she'd come too far to turn back now and she wasn't going to lose her husband.

HEAVEN LEFT THE CHURCH and rolled to Wicker Park to hit up a few boutiques; she wanted to find something extra-sexy to wear for her husband. She was going to update her entire wardrobe piece by piece with seductive outfits that she knew would keep her husband's eyes and hands on her. She bought lingerie from G-Spot and then headed to Akira, where she saw a couple dresses that would be perfect for clubbing but which were not exactly what she had in mind. Then she went to Scoop NYC to check out what they had.

Heaven immediately fell in love with a yellow Diane von Furstenberg Andrina wrap dress. Another woman fell in love with the dress at the same time. They both thumbed through the racks, searching for their size, clearly on a mission but politely respecting each other's space. That is until they figured out that they were both looking for the same size and there was only one left.

"Dibs," Heaven said with a laugh.

"Uh-uh," the woman replied. "We touched it at the same time." She started laughing, too.

"You don't understand. I *need* this dress," Heaven explained. "I've been dreaming of this exact dress in this exact color and style. I have to wear it to dinner tonight with my husband."

"I'm going to Miami, honey. I need this dress more. This dress can't fully be appreciated in Chicago and besides, it's going to be a little cool tonight. You don't want to wear lemon yellow right now, do you?" the woman retorted.

"Yes, I do." Heaven laughed.

"There's only one way to settle this. We'll both have to try the dress on and see who it looks better on."

"Okay," Heaven agreed. "Let's do this. Because I can guarantee that this dress is going to look better on me. No disrespect."

"None taken. But you'll see that it's gonna look like it was made just for me once I put it on."

The two ladies went into the fitting room, one after the other. Each modeled the dress for the customers and clerks. Heaven sighed when she saw her reflection.

"Okay, so you were right," she told the woman. "It does look better on you."

"The lime green one will look better on you. Trust me," the woman said.

"You think?" Heaven asked.

"Yes," the woman told her with a smile. She looked at their audience, who'd been enjoying the impromptu fashion show. "Don't you think?" The crowd nodded yes so Heaven got the dress and put it on.

"Now, that's you," the woman said, complimenting Heaven when she emerged from the dressing room.

"I've gotta admit it. You're right," Heaven said. She turned to the woman and extended her hand. "I can't believe that we've been fighting over this dress all this time and we don't even know each other's names. Where are my manners? My name is Heaven," she said. "Heaven Diaz."

The woman extended her hand and shook Heaven's.

"I'm Gloria," she said. "Gloria Cruz. You can call me Glory, though. Everyone does."

"Nice to meet you, Glory," Heaven said. The two ladies went back into the dressing room and changed into their own clothes, then walked to the register to pay for their purchases.

"So you're going to Miami?" Heaven asked Gloria.

"Yes, and I can't wait. I love Miami."

"Me, too. My husband goes there a lot for business but I don't get to tag along as much as I'd like to," Heaven said.

"That's too bad," Gloria said. "I get down there all the time with my girlfriends. You should turn the tables on your husband sometime and come with us," Gloria suggested mischievously.

"That would blow his mind. I should take you up on

your offer," Heaven said, imagining herself on South Beach having the time of her life with a bunch of fun-loving girls. She was starting to feel better about things already. Not an hour had passed since she'd wished she had more friends, and here one was.

"Well, you're going to have to do it soon. I've got a confession to make. I just found out this morning that I'm expecting a baby, so I'm gonna make a trip down before I start to show."

"Congratulations!" Heaven enthused. "Think I can have the yellow dress once your belly gets too big?" Heaven joked.

"Nah," Gloria said. "I told you that yellow is just not your color. But why don't we exchange numbers," Gloria suggested. Heaven agreed and they beamed each other's information to their respective phones.

"Hey, are you busy right now?" Heaven asked. "I was going to grab a cup of coffee. Wanna come with?"

"I'd love to," Gloria said and followed Heaven to her car.

GLORIA AND HEAVEN WENT to a little coffeehouse and bakery and grabbed a table. Gloria couldn't believe her luck, running into her lover's wife so randomly, but Gloria didn't really believe in coincidence when it came to her Rico. Everything that happened with him was destiny or fate. The fact that she'd outshined Heaven in a dress that she didn't really even like but that Heaven loved was further proof for Gloria that she and Rico were meant for each other.

The fact of the matter was Gloria clocked Heaven the minute she set foot in the boutique. She'd seen a picture of her before once, when she snooped through Ricardo's wallet and had committed that face to memory. Gloria smirked at the thought that she finally met her nemesis while shopping for a trip that she was going to take with her husband. Now she was having coffee and eating sweets and chitchatting with her like they were long-lost friends.

Heaven was an open book. She gave up intimate details of her life without provocation or hesitation. She even confided in Gloria about her marital problems. Within an hour, Gloria had more inside information about Heaven than she ever dreamed she would and she was busy calculating how she'd use that information to tear the couple apart. She knew that it was wise to keep her friends close and her enemies even closer and that's precisely what she planned on doing. Soon Rico would be hers and gullible little Heaven was going to help her.

Gloria told Heaven a few things about herself to pull her even deeper into the guise of friendship. She told her about her career as a dancer and her studies in Paris. She weaved tales of the glamorous parties she attended and the stars she worked for. Heaven hung on to every word.

"Your life sounds so exciting. I feel like a country bumpkin compared to you," Heaven confessed.

"Stick with me, *chica*. You say you want to keep your husband at home, right? Well, if there's one thing I know, it's how to hang on to a man. I'll teach you everything that I know."

"I'll bet," Heaven agreed. "You're very beautiful and exotic and sexy. I bet you have men groveling at your feet."

"And so will you. That husband of yours isn't going to know what hit him," Gloria said. Gloria gave Heaven a few pointers and tips to gain and keep her husband's attention.

"Do you think it will work?" Heaven asked.

"Trust me," Gloria replied, a phony smile plastered across her face.

Chapter 6
CONFESSiONS, PART 2

Rico, Kino, Ysette, and Heaven Diaz hit the Chicago streets looking like superstars. Heads turned and Heaven's shapely frame caught the eye of many men. Rico beamed with pride at the dime piece on his arm. He loved it when men coveted his woman; it reaffirmed that he'd chosen wisely. Kino's wife, Ysette, was also a stunner; a biracial black and Puerto Rican beauty, she had the best of both worlds: smooth mocha-colored skin, long curly hair, and the ass of the motherland. The foursome caused quite a stir at the fancy steakhouse they went to, and Heaven could hear people murmuring and asking each other if the group were celebrities.

They stuffed themselves with prime rib and filet mignon and drank endless bottles of champagne before heading back to Rico's house so the men could discuss some pertinent business. The men resigned themselves to Rico's office while the women fixed *mojitos* in the kitchen.

"Where have you been hiding yourself?" Ysette asked her sister-in-law.

"I haven't been hiding, girl, but you know a woman's work is never done. I've been busy with church, and teaching art to the kids. I help Rico with his marketing and advertising designing ads from time to time, too. Other than that, I've just been taking care of him and our home." Heaven smiled. Ysette frowned.

"Girl, you better go out and get you some satisfaction. You'll grow old sitting around waiting for one of the Diaz boys to be a stay-at-home kind of man. You're wasting your time and your youth."

"Rico's not that bad," Heaven said, but she didn't sound convincing, not even to herself. "Besides, I'm very satisfied."

"Please," Ysette replied, taking a hearty gulp of her drink. "You can't fool me. Rico and Kino are cut from the same cloth. Wandering eyes, wandering dicks, and always on the paper chase."

Heaven sputtered a bit on her drink.

"Oh, come on, Heaven," Ysette continued. "You're not that naïve, are you?"

"I'm not naïve at all," Heaven countered.

"You are if you think that your husband is a faithful man," Ysette said, hitting a nerve.

"What are you trying to say, Ysette? Do you know something that I don't?"

"Don't go getting all sensitive on me, Heaven. You're my girl and I love you. But our husbands are no angels. That's all I'm saying. It's nothing you don't already know. You know how our men got the things that they have—"

"Through hard work," Heaven said, interrupting Ysette. Heaven thought about the scale and other things she found in the box and wondered how much Ysette knew about Rico's shady dealings.

"If you want to wear those blinders, then go ahead. I know how it feels to lie to yourself to help make it through the days and nights. But lying to yourself isn't going to soothe you forever. One day, you're going to have to accept reality for what it is. I know because I've gone through the same thing, Heaven. I used to be just like you. I bent over backward to satisfy Kino, because I loved the hell out of him. But then I realized that I was doing too much and that I was expecting way too much. Now, I live in a state of reality. My husband cheats. I've had proof thrown all in my face by several different bitches. But I've got the ring. I've got the last name Diaz. I've got the man and everything that comes with him. I don't stress those sideline hos. And

I enjoy everything that my man has to offer and then some. I take what I want out of life because who knows how long it's going to last."

"It's going to last forever," Heaven said. "Our marriages are till death do us part."

"You say that now," Ysette said to Heaven. "But after a while, shit changes. Your heart will harden. I'm not saying that you won't love your husband, but your feelings will change."

"Ysette . . . your feelings for Kino, have they changed much?" Heaven asked her.

"Heaven, I still love my man with all my heart. But I know the deal. Any man in the lifestyle our husbands are in is going to be approached by women all the time. There are going to be men who don't want to see them on top. There's always going to be something. But that's the price that we pay for being married to ballers. Everything has a sacrifice." Heaven nodded in agreement.

"Ysette, can I ask you a question?"

"Of course."

"Rico and Kino, they aren't involved in anything illegal, are they?" Heaven already knew the answer to that question, but she needed to hear someone say it. That would make things more real for her. Once she knew exactly what she was up against, she'd know how to proceed. Heaven already had a plan in motion to get her husband back from the clutches of other women, but she didn't know how to fight to get her husband back from the clutches of the streets. She was hoping that Ysette would shed some light on the subject. Ysette just gave her a crazy look that spoke volumes.

"Heaven, you're too sweet for your own good," Ysette said.

"So you're saying that they are?" Heaven asked.

"What do *you* think?" Ysette replied.

In Rico's office, the Diaz brothers sat on espresso-colored leather couches and drank from snifters of brandy.

"So how did things go with big man?" Kino asked Rico.

"Man, you know how crazy that motherfucker is. He's ready to go to war already before some shit even pops off."

"Hey, he might have a point. Sometimes the best defense is a good offense. We can shock and awe those Gary motherfuckers with a preemptive strike that lets them know to stay their asses in Indiana."

"Or, we can just keep our eyes open and not call any attention to ourselves or make things worse with unnecessary bloodshed."

"You're not getting soft on me, are you, big brother?"

"Not at all. Just getting older and hopefully smarter."

"What's on your mind, Rico? I can tell you're thinking about a lot of shit."

"Just thinking about the game. You know I love the money, but every time I'm with Heaven, I start to wonder if all this drama is even worth it. Sometimes I get this feeling that if we stay in the game I'm going to lose her. I've got everything a man wants. I don't want to be too greedy and lose everything."

"Greed is good," Kino told his brother.

" 'For the love of money is the root of all evil.' And it's harder for a rich man to pass through the kingdom of heaven than for a camel to walk through the eye of a needle," Rico replied.

"Your wife got you in church now or something?" Kino teased.

"Nah, man. I just can't help but think about how important my family is to me. If anything were to happen to Heaven or to you, I don't know what I would do."

"Where is all this coming from, man?" Kino asked Rico. "It's like, your attitude changed overnight."

"I don't know. I just have the feeling that some shit is about to hit the fan."

"Big brother, we've got everything under control. Be easy."

Chapter 7
CONFRONTATION

LATER THAT NIGHT, HEAVEN thought about the advice her new friend Gloria had given her. Gloria suggested that Heaven be a little more assertive because no man wanted to be married to a doormat. She advised Heaven to stand up for herself and put her foot down. She also advised that Heaven be a little more adventurous in bed and try something new and freaky. Heaven didn't think those things would go over so well with her husband, but a woman like Glory definitely had more experience in the man department than she did so she was willing to try.

Heaven also thought about the things her sister-in-law had said, as well as the things she didn't say. For years, Heaven wanted to believe that everything with Rico was copacetic. Her whole life had been sewn together by that lie and it was like Ysette had yanked that thread and the whole thing was starting to unravel. Heaven didn't want to start a fight, but she had to be brave and willing to take a risk if she was going to keep her marriage intact.

"Rico, honey," Heaven asked him after Ysette and Kino left and they lay in bed together. "You love me, don't you?"

"Of course. You know you're *mi vida*."

"You say that, but you never spend any time with me," Heaven continued.

"Heaven, what are you talking about? We were together last night, this morning, and tonight. I bought you this ring," he said, holding up her hand. "I thought we had squashed this."

"I still have questions. I want to know where you are all the nights you spend away."

"Heaven, you know where I am."

"I know where you say you are, but I have no real idea where you are or what you're doing."

"Don't you trust me?" Rico looked hurt.

Heaven didn't respond.

"You do trust me, don't you?" Rico repeated.

"Rico, you're my husband. Up until today, I've felt like I didn't have a choice but to trust you. But lately you've done some things that are making it very hard."

"Until today? What happened today?" Rico asked.

Heaven wanted to mention what she'd found in his car but couldn't find the words.

"Honestly, I wonder if there's any satisfying you," Rico said angrily.

"You wonder if you can satisfy me? You've got some nerve. I wonder if *I* have what it takes to satisfy *you*. You were gone three nights last week, and four the week before," Heaven snapped.

"Where do you think the money to pay for this house comes from? You think all this just materializes? I have to work," Rico said emphatically.

"All night long? The dealership closes at nine. I'm not stupid, you know," Heaven retorted.

"I'm the *owner* of Diaz Brothers Import Auto. That means that I don't punch in or out. When I'm not selling, I'm networking." Rico clenched his jaw angrily.

"That's fine. I understand that. But why is it that you can't come home?" Heaven asked. She wasn't sure if his absences were due to illegal business or another woman or both, but she was going to find out.

"Why should I come home when all you're going to do is nag me to death," Rico said.

"That is not fair. I let you do whatever you want, however you want, and I never say a word."

"You pout enough, though. That's just as bad."

Heaven and Rico stared at each other. *This isn't going the way I planned at all,* Heaven thought to herself.

"Heaven, I need to get some rest. I would have liked to have made love to my wife before going to sleep, but from your attitude I can see that that isn't going to happen."

Heaven sighed and threw her arm around her husband. It was time to back down. She didn't want things to get any worse than they already were.

"I'm sorry, baby. It's just that I miss you so much. I love you and I trust you. But more than that, I need you." Heaven reached over to her husband's side of the bed and stroked his shoulder. "I'm not trying to stress you, I swear I'm not."

Ricardo rolled over and looked at his beautiful wife. He cradled her face in his hands and kissed her. She kissed him back with a passion she was sure Rico didn't expect. Heaven was determined to put it on her husband. She didn't want to go into the streets and "find some satisfaction" as her sister-in-law Ysette had suggested. She wanted him to stay at home with her of his own free will and she was going to use everything in her power to ensure that that happened . . . the old-fashioned way. She'd start with that and work on getting him out of the streets later.

Heaven got on top of her husband and began to kiss his chest, making her way down between his legs. Rico stopped her short.

"What are you doing?" he asked, alarmed.

"What does it look like?" she asked him.

"Heaven, baby. You don't have to do that," Rico stated. He felt uncomfortable with the thought of his angelic wife with his cock in her mouth. She was a good girl and shouldn't do things like that.

"I want to," Heaven said. "I want to please you."

"No, Heaven," he said.

"But you're my husband. Nothing that we do together is wrong. Nothing," she said suggestively. Heaven began to stroke Rico's penis, but it wouldn't get erect. She tried and tried to arouse him, attempting to put his manhood in her mouth. Each time she tried, Ricardo pushed her head away.

"You don't want me," Heaven whined, tears beginning to stream down her face.

"It's not that, baby, it's just—"

Heaven silenced him with a glare. "What's her name?" she asked.

"What?" Ricardo asked her with a stunned look on his face. Heaven had caught him off guard.

"What's—her—name?" Heaven repeated, this time

much louder, pronouncing each syllable with the staccato rhythm of gunshots.

"I don't know what you're talking about," Rico stated, and then pushed Heaven aside, rolled over, and shut his eyes.

You bastard! Heaven thought as she lay there in bed next to Ricardo, fuming. Then she thought, *Why am I keeping this all inside?*

Heaven tapped Rico on the shoulder roughly.

"Wake up!" she yelled.

"What, Heaven?" Rico responded gruffly.

"I'm not done," she said. "We're going to talk this thing out."

"What is there to talk out?" Rico asked.

"I found something today," Heaven admitted.

"You found something? Heaven, can't this wait until morning?"

"No, it can't. I don't think that the fact that my husband is a common criminal can wait any longer," Heaven blurted.

"Common criminal?" Rico sat up in bed.

"Yeah. You're a dope pusher, aren't you?" Heaven asked angrily.

"What would make you say something like that?" Rico looked shocked.

"I drove the Jag today. I was putting your dirty clothes in the trunk and I found your little packages. I opened one of the boxes and found your paraphernalia. Tell me, Rico, how long has this been going on beneath my nose? How long have you been pushing poison in our community?" Heaven was on the verge of tears.

"Heaven, you have no idea what you're talking about," Rico stated firmly.

"I know what a scale with white powder residue on it and a money counter are for. And I guess that plastic wrap and Vaseline is used to wrap up your poison."

"You need to be quiet, Heaven, and go to bed because right now you sound crazy." Rico laid back down and pulled the sheets around him. Heaven yanked the sheets back.

"I sound crazy?" she asked incredulously.

"Yes," Rico said, once again pulling the sheets around him. Heaven yanked them away again. Rico sat up and glared at her angrily.

"Don't try to game me. Tell me what that stuff is for!" Heaven demanded.

"You're going to feel stupid when I tell you," Rico said, shaking his head.

"I'm waiting," Heaven said.

"That stuff was left in the trunk of another rental. Someone rented a whip and it was theirs. I brought it with me to get rid of it safely. I didn't want to just put it in the Dumpster behind my place of business. Kino has it now and he's going to make sure that it gets destroyed properly. That's what we were in my office talking about tonight. We're really concerned about things like that happening again."

"You expect me to believe that someone just left that in the car?" Heaven frowned at Rico.

"Yes," Rico answered with a straight face.

"Why? Why should I believe you?" Heaven asked.

"Because it's the truth!" Rico shouted.

"Why would anyone do that?" Heaven continued to probe Rico for answers.

"I can think of a few reasons. Maybe they forgot it was there. Maybe they realized they couldn't take it on the plane with them. I don't know for sure because it isn't mine, and I damn sure don't want to question the person who rented the car about it. There's no telling what kind of shit a person like that is into. I don't want any part of it," Rico explained.

"Swear to me, Rico. Swear that everything you've said is the truth," Heaven demanded.

"Heaven, I swear on my life that I'm not lying. I'd never sell drugs. I know how you feel about that. I feel the same way. Drugs have not only destroyed this country, but Panama as well. I owe it to my people to be a better role model, to be a positive person. I owe that to you as your husband."

Heaven looked at Rico. He seemed so sincere. But Ysette suggested that the Diaz brothers were involved in more than met the eye. However, she didn't say specifically that it was drugs. Maybe their illegal activity was something else altogether, like buying stolen cars or something like that. Not like that would be a good thing, but it was definitely better than selling drugs.

"Heaven, I know I've been messing up lately. I know you have your reasons to doubt me. But you've got to get over it. Without trust, we have nothing. Our marriage means everything to me and I'd never do anything to jeopardize that. Never." Rico pulled Heaven into his arms. "Let's go to sleep, baby, okay? It's been a long day and we both could use the rest."

"I guess you're right," Heaven said, and snuggled under the sheets with her husband.

Chapter 8
THE HiT

"Yo, MAN, WE GOT hit."

Ricardo rubbed his eyes and switched his cell phone from one ear to the other as he sat up in bed. The phone rang at an ungodly hour and the news he received from his brother wasn't good.

"What did you say?" Rico asked Kino.

"I said we got hit."

"What exactly do you mean by that?" Rico was still half asleep and needed clarification.

"I'm saying that some motherfuckers ran up in one of our stash spots and took some product and some money," Kino explained.

"Which spot?" Rico asked.

"Man, our joint over in the hundreds. They held Ms. Watkins at gunpoint," Kino said.

Ms. Watkins was the middle-aged woman who owned the home that they stored a bulk of their drugs and money in. She had been Hyckef's babysitter when he was younger and her oldest son used to be a player in the streets before he got killed in a shoot-out at a nightclub. Ms. Watkins knew the dope game in and out and was known for her ill temper and ever-ready trigger finger; she'd bust shots at the postman if she thought he was trying to run up in her spot. She had mad respect in the "Wild Wild Hundreds," as her neighborhood was called. No one had *ever* messed with her . . . until tonight.

"Are you serious?" Rico was in a state of shock. In all the time they had been running their drug enterprise, they hadn't had to deal with fools coming out of pocket. They had a rep on the streets and people didn't cross the line. Sure, every now and then a stickup kid trying to make a name for himself tried to pull off a petty robbery, but this was some real shit.

"Yeah, man, dead-ass." Kino's voice was filled with anger. Rico knew his brother was ready to set it off.

"How much did they get?" Rico needed to assess the damage and work out numbers in his head. He would keep his mind focused on their paper and let his brother and Hyckef handle the issuance of street justice.

"Ten bricks and about a hundred thou in cash."

Yeah, this shit is real serious, Rico said to himself.

"Who the fuck did it?" Rico asked.

"You know who the fuck did. It was that motherfucker Black."

"He rollin' with a crew like that?"

"He did that shit on the dolo. Slipped in her crib while she was sleeping."

"What about her dog?" Ms. Watkins had a crazy-mean blue pit bull that had a bite as severe as his bark.

"That crazy motherfucker poisoned the dog. And he by-passed her alarm system. He was on some straight *Mission Impossible* shit."

"Yeah, but in the meantime that cat got away with a mil worth of our shit. We can't let that fly. We've got to send a message."

"Fuck a message. We got to off that motherfucker. If we let him live, other cats will see us as marks."

"That's precisely the message I had in mind, *hermano.* Handle it," Rico said and hung up.

"Was that your bitch?" Heaven asked Rico as he lay back down.

"What?" Rico asked. He was shocked as hell. Heaven never used profanity.

"I said, was that your bitch calling you to find out where you are?"

"No, Heaven. That was Kino. Damn, I swear every time I think we got beyond our problems you bring them back up. Now me and Kino got some real shit going on, so spare me, all right?" Rico felt every muscle in his body tense up as the stress of his street situation and the stress of his home situation started to mount. He needed relief. He pulled the covers back and sat back up in bed. He swung his legs over the side and got out.

"Where are you going?" Heaven asked.

"I have to go to the office and work on some things."

"At this hour? It's four-thirty in the morning."

"Yeah, well, this business can't wait," Rico said.

"Fine. Go to your whore," Heaven spat.

Be careful what you ask for, Rico thought.

BLACK SAT IN HIS kitchen with the spoils of his stickup spread out across the table. He had nearly a mil in coke in front of him, not to mention the cash he took. He'd wanted to kill that old busybody Ms. Watkins, but he needed to leave her alive so that she could tell the Diaz brothers that Black and his G.I. Boys weren't to be taken lightly. He'd even made sure to run the caper solo, so that the Panamanian brothers would recognize that they were no match for him. They'd be out of business by the end of the week if their entire organization was as easy to infiltrate as Ms. Watkins.

Black reckoned that the next move he made wouldn't be to hit one of the Diaz brothers' stash houses; he was going to take over the operation. When the time was right he was going to rain a bloodstorm on Chicago the likes of which had never before been seen. His attack was going to be swift, brutal, and merciless.

As he chopped up, cut, and weighed the coke from the kilos into ounce-size packets, Black thought about all the money he was about to make from the score. It was pure profit. He smiled, satisfied with himself. The robbery he'd pulled off had been just the beginning. He was on his way now, straight to the top of the food chain, and he was going to devour the Diaz brothers in the process.

"Papi, is everything okay?" Gloria asked Rico when he showed up at her doorstep at the crack of dawn.

"No, Glory, it isn't," Rico said solemnly.

"Sit down and relax. Let me fix you a drink," Gloria offered, leading Rico to the sofa. She went to the bar and poured him a snifter of cognac and brought it back to him. Then she sat at his feet and removed his shoes. Gloria began to rub and massage Rico's feet.

"Tell me what's going on," she cooed.

"We got hit today," Rico confessed. "A couple of hours ago this cat from Gary named Black hit one of our stash houses. He got away with ten bricks and some dough."

"What?" Gloria asked in shock, doing the math in her mind. "That's a lot of money," she told Rico.

"You damn straight it is."

"And I know you can't let that shit ride," she told him, making her way up his calves with her magic fingers. She rolled and kneaded his flesh, working out the kinks and knots of tension.

"No. I didn't want to go to war but I don't have a choice. Bigger beefs have been started for less."

Gloria unbuckled Rico's pants and pulled them off. "You're right, Papi, but I can't help but worry. This is serious."

"Don't worry, Glory. We've got it under control. Black won't be a problem for anyone soon."

"Good," Gloria said, pulling off Rico's boxers. "I'd die if anything happened to you."

Gloria began to caress and stroke him with her hands and mouth until Rico's mind was far from war. Gloria wanted to tell Rico that she was carrying his child but decided against it. He had enough on his mind. Instead, Gloria took him into her mouth and proceeded to take Rico's troubles away. She sucked him until he was ready to release and then straddled him. Gloria mounted Rico and began to ride, swiveling her hips up, down, and in circles.

"How's that feel to you, Papi?" Gloria asked. Rico sucked her breasts as she rode him and Gloria threw her head back with pleasure each time his tongue touched her nipples.

"It's good, baby. It's just what I needed," Rico said as Gloria worked her magic on him.

"I love you, Papi," Gloria said as she bounced on top of him. "Tell me you love me," she ordered. Ricardo didn't answer.

"*Dímelo*," she commanded in Spanish. She ground her hips hard against him, using her muscles to clench him within her walls. She could feel him throbbing inside of her and it felt so good that her head started to spin slightly.

"I love you, Gloria," Rico said. His words pushed Gloria over the edge and she began to come, working her hips forcefully now until Rico came, too.

"I love you, Papi," Gloria repeated. "I'm here for you through thick and thin. Remember that," she told him, looking into his eyes.

"I know, Glory," Rico said. "Now, why don't you run some water for me to take a nice hot shower and while I'm in you can cook something for me to eat."

Gloria smiled. "Just tell me what you want."

"Surprise me," Rico told her, and Gloria set off to do just that.

Rico watched her ass jiggle as she walked away and immediately felt like an asshole. He'd spent the better part of the past two days trying to convince his wife that he was faithful and legit, yet there he was, back with Gloria and trying to figure out how to squash an impending drug war. He knew how hurt Heaven would be if she knew the truth about the things he did, which was why he lied to her. He also knew he was dead wrong for his behavior, but he couldn't help himself. Money and pussy were his weaknesses and he knew that it would be a long time before he could be strong enough to be the man his wife needed him to be.

Chapter 9
A NEW BEGiNNiNG

HEAVEN GOT UP EARLIER than usual the next morning. She didn't even bother to bathe or brush her teeth. She got in her car and headed to Logan Square to visit her family.

"Heaven, what a surprise!" her mother, Mrs. Rivera, said with a huge smile when she opened the door and saw her baby girl standing there.

"Hi, Mami," Heaven said softly. "This isn't a bad time, is it?"

"Never!" her mother replied. "Come on in here."

"Heaven!" Heaven's father scooped her up in his arms and attempted to twirl her around.

"Papi, you'll throw your back out trying to pick me up," Heaven warned.

"I keep forgetting you're not a little girl anymore," Mr. Rivera said with a chuckle. "And I keep forgetting that I'm not a young man!"

Heaven laughed dryly.

"Heaven, are you okay?" he asked. "You don't look so good."

"I'm okay, Papi," Heaven lied.

"No, you aren't," her *papi* said. "But I guess it's a girl thing, huh? I'll leave you and your mother to talk," he said. "I'm going to take a walk." Heaven and her mother smiled at him as he left.

"Mamá!" Mrs. Rivera shouted. "*Ven aqui!*"

Heaven's grandmother came into the kitchen. She smiled a mile wide when she saw her grandchild.

"Hi, Abuelita," Heaven said.

"Heaven, what's wrong?" she asked.

"Why does everyone keep asking me that?" Heaven complained.

"Because we know you. Now spill it," Mrs. Rivera said sternly.

"Mami, Abuelita, I don't know what to do. Rico—"

"He didn't hit you, did he?" Heaven's grandmother asked. She reached into the drawer and pulled out a butcher knife. "Because if he did, I will personally cut his cojones off!"

"Mamá!" Heaven's mother exclaimed.

"I'm just saying," Abuelita replied.

"I think Rico is unfaithful," Heaven said. Abuelita and Mrs. Rivera laughed.

"What man isn't?" Abuelita asked. "They're all guided by their peepees, you know. Get yourself a big, sharp knife and slice it off if you want him to be faithful," she said, then howled with laughter. Mrs. Rivera walked over to her mother and took the knife out of her hand.

"Mamá, enough with the cutting of the peepees and cojones, okay?" Mrs. Rivera laughed at her mother.

"I'm just saying," Abuelita said once more and this time all three women laughed. Heaven's laughter quickly morphed into tears. Abuelita wrapped her arms around her granddaughter and hugged her close to her bosom.

"There, there, that's my girl. You just go on and let it all out," she said in an attempt to soothe her. "Your mother cried to me just like you are when she was your age."

"You did?" Heaven asked, looking at her mother through tear-soaked eyes. "Papi cheated on you?"

"All men cheat," Mrs. Rivera said. "Especially our men. It's the machismo, you know. But that doesn't mean that they don't love us. It's just their way."

"But Mami, Rico said vows," Heaven complained.

"We all make promises we can't keep from time to time," Abuelita said.

"Yes, to other people. But shouldn't we take the promises we make to God more seriously?" Heaven asked her.

"Sure! But God knows where, when, and how we will fall short. You just have to stick it out and keep the faith. Pray for your husband."

"I'm tired of everyone telling me that!" Heaven snapped. "Why do I have to do all the work? It's not fair."

"Life isn't fair," Mrs. Rivera said. "But life is all we have. Cherish the life you have with Rico. Do what you can to keep your family together."

Heaven dried her tears with the back of her hand. It was obvious that no one understood how she felt. And if they couldn't understand how she felt about Rico cheating, there was no way they'd understand her other fears.

"I'm going to go for a walk to clear my head," she announced to her mother and grandmother.

"Heaven," Mrs. Rivera called out to her daughter as she headed out the front door.

"Leave her be, *nena*. This is hard for her. These young girls have their own crazy ideas about what love is. But she will learn," Heaven heard her grandmother tell her mother on her way out.

HEAVEN STROLLED LEISURELY THROUGH her old hood. She waved at some of her old neighbors and thought about the good old days when her life was so much simpler. Then she passed her old church and felt angrier than she'd felt in a long, long time. She pulled her rosary out of her purse and threw it in the gutter in front of the church.

"I've always done what you wanted," Heaven said out loud, looking at the sky. She didn't care if she looked like a lunatic. She had beef with the man upstairs. "I know I sound like a brat, but what did I do to deserve this?"

Just as Heaven was having her angry little tirade against God, a transient woman who was clearly mentally disturbed walked past her. The woman, who was cloaked in rags and had a pungent odor, stopped in front of Heaven and twitched a little. Then she looked up at the sky along with Heaven and started to yell, as well.

"That's right, that's right!" the woman shouted. "Stop fucking with us. We can see you."

Heaven looked at the woman and immediately felt like shit. Here she was complaining about some *man* and letting him take her through all kinds of changes when there were people out there with *real* problems. The woman smiled a toothless smile at Heaven and Heaven's heart melted. She reached into her purse and pulled out a twenty-dollar bill. She handed it to the woman.

"Go buy some food," she said to the woman. "Okay?" The woman looked at her, confused.

"As a matter of fact, go buy some new clothes, too, and

try and find a place to stay." Heaven extracted a hundred-dollar bill from her bag and handed it to the woman, too. The woman was crazy, but not too crazy to see that there was cold hard cash in front of her. She quickly snatched up the bills and put them inside her shirt and looked at Heaven with tears in her eyes.

"God bless you," the woman said before toddling off down the street screaming obscenities.

God has blessed me, Heaven thought. So much. I'm alive, I'm healthy, and I have a home to go to. I have family and friends. Instead of thanking God, I've been complaining that it isn't enough. I expect Him to make my life perfect. I thought if I had the perfect husband or the perfect child, my life would be perfect, too. But maybe my life is just how He wants it. Maybe these marital problems will ultimately make Rico and me a stronger couple. Maybe there's a reason I haven't conceived a child yet. Maybe I should cherish the time that I have to myself or use it to further glorify God. Other women have to check in with and report to their husbands. I have money and freedom. Today, I'm going to start enjoying them both.

Heaven extracted her rosary from the gutter and pulled out her cell phone and punched in her sister-in-law's phone number, but got her voice mail. Then Heaven had an idea. She'd call her new friend Glory, the woman from the boutique. Maybe they could grab a quick bite to eat.

"Hello, Glory, this is Heaven. Remember me?" Heaven said when Gloria answered.

"I remember you. How are you, girl?" Gloria said, as if she were happy to hear from Heaven.

"I'm okay. It's just that it's a nice day and it's finally getting kind of warm outside. It's too pleasant to stay inside and I was wondering if you'd like to grab some lunch with me," Heaven suggested.

"I'd love to," Gloria enthused. "What time did you have in mind?"

Heaven and Gloria decided to meet at a Thai restaurant near the Chicago River in a few hours. In the meanwhile, Heaven decided to go home and get presentable and then engage in one of her favorite pastimes: shopping. First, she rolled through a hip-hop lifestyle shop called Phli in her Hyde Park neighborhood. She'd seen the store several times but had never stopped in before. The mohawked owner, Dave Jeff, gave her a tour of the store and she saw that his unique clothes and gym shoes were seen on rappers like Lupe Fiasco, Common, and Kanye West. She instantly fell in love with the one-of-a-kind merchandise.

She bought herself a pair of pink-and-gold Nikes that Dave assured her no one else in the city would have. She also bought Rico a couple of pairs of custom Nikes and a Phli logo shirt that had Austrian crystals all over it. Then Heaven stopped at Dr. Wax to look at their music selection. She loved strolling through the aisles and aisles of vinyl and CDs, scoping out favorites from her childhood and discovering artists from other countries who had cool, eclectic vibes.

After Dr. Wax, she headed to another one of her favorite boutiques closer to her final destination, Breathe. She decided to park her car in a parking deck and take a cab to the restaurant after she did major damage to Ricardo's credit card at Breathe. The owner, Mia, had exquisite taste and always held the best of the new stuff in Heaven's size for her. Heaven selected her favorites and had Mia hold them until her return, than headed to meet Gloria.

GLORIA MARVELED AT HOW easy getting close to Heaven was going to be, and she began to devise multiple plans on the spot. There were so many ways she could play this, so many ways she could use her lover's wife to her advantage. All Gloria had to be careful about was keeping her schemes from Ricardo.

At the restaurant, the two women greeted each other with a hug that looked and felt sincere, at least it probably did to Heaven. Gloria wanted to snap Heaven's rib cage when she put her arms around her and rip out her heart. The ladies were seated and given water and tea, then they looked over the menu. They both decided to sample from the lunch buffet, and after they'd gotten their plates they got comfortable and started to chitchat.

Gloria asked Heaven a million and one questions, hanging on to her every reply. She wanted to know all that she could, and Heaven, as predicted, spewed information forth like a geyser. Gloria couldn't believe her luck when Heaven started talking about her relationship with Rico and asking for her advice again.

"What would you do if you thought your husband was cheating on you?" Heaven asked Gloria.

"You told me that things were rough between you, but do you really think your husband is cheating on you?" Gloria replied, not answering Heaven's question.

"Yeah. He's always gone overnight when he really doesn't have to be. And last night he left in the middle of the night claiming that he was having problems with his business. It was just another one of his excuses that don't hold water."

"Did you try the advice I gave you the last time?" Gloria asked.

"Yeah. I stood up for myself and I even tried to give him a blow job."

"Well, what happened?"

"He rejected me," Heaven admitted, dejected.

"Try harder," Gloria suggested. "You can't give up without a fight."

"That's what I thought, but I guess I'm not as tough as I thought I was. I'm so stressed out I don't know what I'm going to do. I swear, I feel like any minute now I'm going to snap and just go postal."

"Then go postal. Why hold shit inside? Let me tell you something about men. They respect a woman who calls them on their bullshit. Or better yet, ignore him. Become totally self-centered. You sound like you're Suzy Homemaker."

"So, what's wrong with that?"

"Nothing, if you want to keep on going through what you're going through. Get a job or something. Just do whatever it takes to show him that you are capable of living without him. Assert your independence. You don't really want to tend to his needs twenty-four/seven/three sixty-five, do you? What about *your* needs? I'm telling you, get ghost or focus on you instead of focusing on him so much, and he'll come around."

Heaven sighed and nodded in agreement.

"I was kind of thinking along those lines a little earlier today. I hadn't planned on ignoring him, just doing things for me."

"Go big or go home, that's what I always say. Don't just

do you, show him that you're a modern woman who doesn't have to sit around and wait for a man."

"Think it will work?" Heaven asked Gloria.

"I know it will," Gloria said, all the while laughing inside at the mischief she was causing. "The way I see it, this is all your husband's fault. He's crazy to ignore you. I mean, I barely know you, but you seem to be the total package. You're beautiful, smart, and nice. If he doesn't appreciate that, find someone who does."

"Now you sound just like my sister-in-law Ysette," Heaven said.

"Well, there you have it. Two women have told you to go out and do you."

"It just seems so selfish."

"So what? He's being selfish, too. You can show him much better than you can tell him that you won't stand for his shit anymore."

"I could never do that," Heaven said. "I love my husband too much."

"Fuck that. Sure you could. Forget about loving your husband. You *need* to start loving yourself."

Chapter 10
A PERSONAL GUARANTEE

BLACK DROVE HIS BLACK Chevy Impala into the Miller Beach section of Gary. Tucked away in the Indiana sand dunes, few people knew that such an upscale neighborhood existed in a city with a reputation like Gary. There were million-dollar mansions that overlooked the shores of Lake Michigan and stately upper-middle-class homes with sprawling yards.

As he drove down Lake Street and passed the public library, he noticed a black Mercedes pull out and drive directly behind him. He made a few turns to confirm that he was being followed. He was. But Black wasn't stressed about it, not one bit. He stopped at a stop sign and the Mercedes swerved and pulled up next to him. He could see that the men inside had weapons. He stared directly at them and didn't move. The men opened fire.

• • •

"THAT MOTHERFUCKER GOT AWAY," Hyckef told Rico. They were meeting at the auto dealership after hours to discuss their problem with Black. A hit had been placed on him, but there had been difficulty executing it.

"What the fuck do you mean, he got away?" Rico asked incredulously. Very rarely did he lose his temper and totally blow up, but he was on the verge of a thermonuclear meltdown. He wanted the problem with Black handled. "How hard is it to roll up on someone and blast their ass?"

"That's a slick-ass motherfucker," Hyckef continued. "His hooptie is bulletproof."

"Yo, get the fuck outta here!"

"I'm serious. We shot like hell at that damn Impala and ain't shit happen. That bastard smiled at us as he drove away."

"You're going to have to come harder and smarter. Someone needs to catch his ass on foot and off guard. I want a bullet through his fucking head. I'm going to have a hard time focusing on the business I have to take care of in Miami thinking about this shit. Handle it!"

"I got you, man, and I want the same thing. Just go on and go to Miami. I personally guarantee you that when you come back that motherfucker Black will be six feet under."

Chapter 11
MiAMi HEAT

RICARDO AND GLORIA STEPPED off the G4 Ricardo chartered at the Kendall-Tamiami airport and stepped into a waiting fiery orange-colored Lotus Elise.

"This car is so hot," Gloria enthused.

"Just like you, baby," Ricardo said, holding her hand.

The couple checked into the Setai, a gorgeous boutique hotel that blended Art Déco style with Asian influences. Gloria's eyes tripled in size as they stepped into the ten-thousand-foot rooftop penthouse. She spun around in a circle and then ran giddily from room to room, oohing and aahing at the pool and panoramic views.

"Oh Papi, this is so wonderful," Gloria told him.

"You like it?" he asked.

"I love it!" Gloria gushed.

"Then prove it," Rico said with a sly smile.

Gloria stepped out of her clothes and stood before Ricardo. She began to wind her hips sensuously as she removed her panties and then her bra.

"You were always the best dancer I've ever seen," Ricardo told her, licking his lips.

Gloria ran her hands over her body and walked slowly toward Rico. She kissed him passionately, rubbing her body against him.

"Tell me what you want me to do, Papi. Tonight I'm going to be your every fantasy."

Ricardo led Gloria onto the rooftop deck and sat down in a chair.

"First I want you to dance for me," he ordered. Gloria began to move and shimmy, maintaining eye contact with Rico the entire time. Rico enjoyed his little floor show for a few moments and then continued his demands. "Now get on your knees and crawl to me."

For a nanosecond, Gloria thought that his request was a tad bit degrading, but she instinctively did it anyway. She would do absolutely anything to satisfy Rico.

"Now open your mouth and I want you to suck it for

me." Gloria acquiesced and began to give him head. Rico fondled her breasts as she did, taking in a nice view of her full and rounded backside as her head bobbed up and down. "That's right, girl. Suck it for Papi."

Rico felt his scrotum tighten and pushed Gloria's head away. "Not yet, Glory. I want to fuck that pussy," he said. He led Gloria to a railing where she could take in the view of the beach and ocean. Bending her over slightly, he entered her from behind and began to rock against her. Gloria rocked back, moaning as she felt him fill her completely. Gloria had never felt a sensation so intense before, being in such an amazing suite with the love of her life, looking out at the Atlantic Ocean. She had a massive orgasm until tears flowed down her face.

"Oh Papi, I love you so much," she yelled as she came.

"I love you, too, Glory," Rico said, and followed suit with a powerful orgasm of his own.

"Do you really?" Gloria asked him as they detached themselves and held each other under the Miami sky.

"Yes, I do," Ricardo assured her, kissing her on the forehead. "You're my Chula."

"Good, because I have something to tell you," Gloria said, smiling at Rico. She knew she'd found the perfect moment to reveal her news to him. They'd just finished making passionate love and he was holding her close, telling her how he felt for her. They were away from every-one and everything that could oppose them. Gloria took a deep breath and opened her mouth to speak but no sound came out.

"What is it?" he asked. "You know you can tell me any-thing."

"I'm pregnant," Gloria blurted.

"You're *what*?" Rico stood back and held Gloria away from him at arm's length.

"I'm pregnant. I'm having your baby," Gloria said, grin-ning.

"How do I know that it's mine?" Ricardo asked. Gloria's smile disappeared.

"What?" Gloria screeched incredulously. "I can't be-lieve you would even twist your mouth to say some bullshit like that to me. You know that you're the only one."

"I know you *say* that I'm the only one, but how do I re-ally *know* that?" Rico asked, looking at her dubiously.

"Ricardo, we've been together since we were kids. I'm telling you on everything that this is your baby. I love you with all my heart and soul. Another man couldn't get close enough to this body to experience it. I have no doubts. This is you," Gloria said, pointing at her stomach.

"Well, what do you plan on doing?" Ricardo asked her, with the worst possible response a man can have when a woman tells him that she's carrying his child. It always, always pisses the woman off, which is precisely what happened. Gloria began to breathe heavily and her neck was rotating a mile a minute.

"What do *I* plan on doing? Don't you mean *we*? We're in this together," Gloria snapped.

"Fine then. What do you think *we* should do about it?" Rico asked.

"What do you think I want? I want to have it," Gloria said. "This is a baby conceived in love. I'm not going to kill it."

"Gloria, you can't have this baby," Rico protested. "I'm a married man."

"And?" Gloria asked, putting her hands on her hips. "You can fuck me, but you can't handle the responsibility that comes with it?"

"A baby wasn't supposed to come with this. But I can handle any responsibility," Rico told her. "Look, I'm not going to pretend that I'm happy about this."

Gloria's face dropped and her stomach sank.

"I can't believe you just said that to me," she cried. "We've known each other forever; I'm not some strange slut that got knocked up. I'm Glory, your Chula, the woman that you love, and now I'm going to be the mother of your child."

"I can't talk about this right now," Rico said, turning to walk away.

"Where are you going?" Gloria asked him, panic-stricken.

"Out," Ricardo said coldly. "I need to clear my mind."

"Oh, no you don't," Gloria said. "You're not going to turn your back on me and walk away. No fucking way!" Gloria grabbed Rico by the arm and he shook her off violently.

"Don't touch me, Gloria," Rico spat angrily.

"What?" Gloria shrieked. Gloria reached out and grabbed Rico's arm again and this time Rico slapped her.

"Oh, hell no!" Gloria said. She balled up her fist and punched him in the eye as hard as she could. In an instant, the two of them were scrapping naked like two savages. Gloria scratched and clawed and hit Rico with all her might. Rico wrapped his hands around Gloria's neck and squeezed. Gloria struggled and gasped for air but couldn't breathe. If she didn't do something quickly, Rico was going to end her life right then and there. Gloria managed to knee Rico in the nuts and she scrambled into a corner.

Gloria felt her face. It was sore and she could taste blood. She touched her lip. It felt like it was three times its normal size. Rico limped over to where Gloria was cowering in the corner.

"You crazy bitch. I ought to kill you!" Before he could

stop himself, he kicked Gloria in the side and spit on her. Gloria screamed in pain and it was as if her screams snapped Rico back to reality. He'd done the unthinkable. He'd struck a woman, something he promised his mother that he would never do. He shook his head in shame, turned quickly on his heels, and left the room.

Tears streamed down Gloria's face and she made no attempt to wipe them away or stop them. Her body shook from the force of her sobs as she watched the so-called love of her life put on his clothes and walk out the door. Gloria rose to her knees, but this time it wouldn't be to service Rico. She looked up at the heavens with her hands clasped in prayer.

"Oh God, this can't be happening. Ricardo didn't just do this to me. He can't walk out on me and this baby. Please God. Please, make it right."

"Oye, primo," Rico said into his cell phone. "Dónde estás?" Rico had called his cousin Ramón, who happened to be his cocaine connection, in a panic. Ramón was older and a true G. They had business to take of but Rico figured he'd ask Ramón's advice on how to handle the situation with Gloria.

"Acércate," Ramón said, letting his cousin know that he was nearby.

"I'm over at the Marlin, man. Hurry up and get here. I gotta talk to you."

"I'm pulling up to the valet now," Ramón told him.

"Man, don't park. We need to talk and ride. I'm coming out."

Ricardo walked outside of the Marlin and greeted his cousin Ramón, who immediately got out of his Bentley Continental and walked around to give his cousin a pound.

"What's going on, cousin?" Ramón asked. The two men got into the car and began to roll down Collins Avenue.

"You know my side chick, Gloria, right? She just told me she's pregnant," Ricardo told his cousin.

"For real?"

"Yeah, man. My wife is going to have a fit."

"Your wife ain't gotta know," Ramón reasoned. "There's no reason to put her through all of that. You've got to protect her."

"Gloria is the type of chick that's gonna blow up my spot. Ain't no way she's not gonna let it be known she's carrying my child."

"Make her get rid of it."

"I may have already helped her do that. We had a fight."

"A fight? You mean like an argument?"

"No, like a fight."

"You hit her?"

"I hit her and then some. It was like, I couldn't control myself. I can't believe what I've done."

"I can't believe you either, man. We weren't raised like that."

"I know, man, and I feel like shit."

Ramón shook his head at his cousin. "What are you going to do? You think that Gloria is going to tell Heaven? Or worse, the police?"

"I don't know."

"Look, you better do whatever it takes to calm this shit down and quick."

"Duh, I already know that. I just don't know what to do," Rico said.

"Focus on making your wife happy when you get back. Let me handle the rest."

"You're not going to kill Gloria, are you?"

"Hell no, man! I'm gonna make sure that she has enough paper to keep her mouth shut."

"I don't think there's enough money in the world."

"Let me worry about that. In the meantime, have fun while you're here. Get your mind off the shit because stressing isn't going to change anything," Ramón said.

"You're right, *primo*," Rico said.

"I know. Now I hate to sound callous, but we gotta handle this business. A'ight?"

"Sure, man," Ricardo said.

Ricardo and Ramón drove to a warehouse in the Sweetwater section of Miami. The warehouse park was practically abandoned, which was good because they had some dirt to do. They pulled up to a loading dock and rolled up the ramp. Ramón flashed the lights. The doors to the warehouse opened slowly and Ramón drove in. A man with an assault rifle rushed to the driver's side. He opened the door for Ramón and he stepped out, straightening his linen suit. Ramón tossed the man his keys.

"How long will it take?" Ramón asked the man with the gun.

"The car will be ready in a couple of hours. We'll load it and the others on the trailer and then they'll be on their way."

"*Bueno*," Ramón said. "What you got for me?" he asked the man with the gun. The man used the rifle to point at a Ferrari Superamerica F1.

"How will that work for you?" he asked.

"That's nice," Ramón replied.

"That's what I thought."

Rico and Ramón headed back to South Beach once they were satisfied that the hundred-kilo shipment was properly hidden in special compartments in the whips that were being transported back to Chicago. Rico was going to clear about five million from the product when all was said and done. Not bad for a day's work. The only thing that was weighing on him was Gloria. He quickly pushed the thought of her out of his mind.

He was in South Beach, land of the beautiful people. There were a million women ready, willing, and available to party with him and his cousin. He didn't need Gloria's nagging, pleading, and crying. He already had a wife. The whole point of having a mistress was to be able to have an escape from his husbandly responsibilities.

Ramón spotted two hotties walking toward the Mansion nightclub on Washington Avenue.

"Take a look at that, *primo*," Ramón said.

"I see it. But are we gonna just look or get the party started?" Rico asked.

"You already know the answer to that, cousin," Ramón replied. "You already know."

Chapter 12

A THiN LiNE BETWEEN LOVE AND HATE

GLORIA CRIED UNCONTROLLABLY ON the floor of the penthouse. Her mind was reeling and she was in excruciating pain that got worse with every passing minute. The sharp, piercing pains in her midsection caused her to double over and curl her body into a ball and rock back and forth. Something was wrong. Very wrong. Then Gloria felt a warm stickiness between her thighs. She looked down and saw blood trickling down her thigh. Gloria panicked. There was no way she could lose the baby. She needed help. She needed Ricardo. She wasn't sure if she loved him anymore or if she hated him, but she didn't know who else to call.

Gloria crawled over to the chair where her purse lay and grabbed her cell phone. She punched in Rico's number and listened to it ring until his voice mail picked up. "Damn," she muttered to herself. She sent Rico a text:

Something is very wrong. I'm hurt pretty bad and I think I may need to go to a hospital. Please hurry back. I need you.

Rico had to come back now. There's no way he'd leave her lying bleeding on the floor. He loved her. He wasn't a total asshole . . . was he?

RICO LOOKED AT HIS cell phone and read the latest incoming text message. He debated whether or not to reply, and then decided not to. If Gloria were truly hurt she'd call an ambulance and he didn't want to be anywhere near her in case the police got involved. He knew it was cowardly and he was dead wrong, but he didn't have a choice in the matter. He had to protect himself and his wife.

Rico focused his attention on the two young women who were standing next to Ramón's car. Ramón had pulled over and began putting his mack down. He didn't have to say or do much. His clothes, jewels, whip, and swagger spoke for themselves. Within seconds the two men had the two gorgeous women on their arms and were headed into Mansion to have a good time.

The club was packed to capacity. Multiplatinum-selling rapper 50 Cent was in the spot, throwing an impromptu celebration in honor of his latest entrepreneurial coup, the highly profitable sale of Glacéau Vitamin Water, in which he was a major investor. The crowd was amped to the fullest because the DJ was bumping tracks from 50's soon-to-be released CD, *Curtis*, and everyone was a certified club banger. Haters were throwing shade, muttering comments like, "That cat ain't all that," while groupies were swarming the VIP section that 50 Cent had commandeered, trying to get a glimpse, a touch, anything from the bodied-up superstar, who took everything in stride.

"Ooh, he is so fine," one of the women who'd joined Ricardo and Ramón whispered to her girlfriend.

"I know. His body is on point. I wonder if he really does have a magic stick," her friend replied, licking her lips.

"If he does, he can hit me with it," her friend bantered.

Rico heard the whole thing but ignored it. He had enough women problems for one night. Besides, all he was trying to do was cut the shorty he picked up so he could momentarily forget his troubles. He didn't care if she fantasized about 50 or her father, as long as she was ready, willing, and able to romp in the sheets with him when the time came.

GLORIA FELT WEAK AND shaky and the cramping and bleeding was getting worse. She knew that she was losing her baby. She wanted to wait for Rico, but she knew that she was betting on a long shot if she expected him to come rushing to her side after the way they fought. She dragged her body to the nightstand and grabbed the phone.

"Front desk, may I help you?" a woman's chipper voice said on the other end.

"Help me. Please help me," Gloria breathed into the phone.

"Are you okay? What's the matter?" the front desk operator asked with concern.

"I need an ambulance. I think I'm having a miscarriage. I'm in the penthouse," Gloria uttered, then passed out.

RICO AND RAMÓN HAD spent a couple hours and a couple thousand dollars in Mansion with the ladies they'd met on Washington.

"Let's go," Rico said to his companion. He was ready to bounce.

"Go where? The party is just getting started," she complained.

"Nah," Rico said. "I got the party right here." He pulled a baggie of coca out of his pocket and flashed it at the girl. She grinned wildly and snaked her arms around him.

"Why didn't you say that you were ready to go?" she quipped. She whispered a few words to her friend, who responded positively, and the foursome settled their tab and left the club.

They rode to one of Ramón's many cribs, a Mediterranean-style villa about three miles from South Beach. Once inside, they wasted no time getting the festivities going. Once they had snorted a few lines of premium white, the women stripped to their underwear and began to make out. Ramón quickly got undressed and stepped in between the women, grabbing their breasts and squeezing their asses as they kissed him all over.

"*Oye, primo*, you better get one of these women. I don't know if I can handle them both," Ramón said to Rico.

But all Rico could think about was Heaven. If she knew what he'd done it would destroy her. He knew that he had to make a change in his life, no matter how hard it was, or he'd lose her forever and that was a thought he couldn't bear. Contrary to his actions, he truly loved his wife, but like so many other men he allowed himself to be led by his dick and by his passion for an old girlfriend. The attention that was lavished on him by both women was addictive but he was going to have to get the monkey off his back, no matter what it took.

SIRENS BLARED AS AN ambulance transported Gloria to a nearby hospital. She cried and wailed all the way there, not just out of physical pain, but out of emotional anguish, as well. She was losing her baby and she knew that there was probably little or nothing that could be done about it. And she had clearly lost her hold on Rico. He should have been happy about their child. He should have never walked out on her. He should have never abandoned her when she needed him the most.

He had proven in one evening that everything he'd said to her for the past fifteen years was bullshit. He didn't love her. If he did, he wouldn't have hit her. If he loved her, he wouldn't have married that simple bitch Heaven. If he loved her, he'd be with her, right by her side holding her hand. The only solace that Gloria felt was that although Rico didn't really love her, he didn't really love Heaven, either. No, a man like Rico only loved one person, and that was himself. Everything he said and everything he did was for his own gain.

As Gloria recovered from the D&C the doctors performed, she realized something else. She didn't love Rico, either. Now that she saw what he was really about, how could she love him? She wasn't some wimpy little pushover like Heaven. She would never allow any man to treat her with such disregard. All the love she'd once felt had been transformed into an entirely different emotion: hate.

Chapter 13
THE BEST-LAiD PLANS

RICARDO WAS FILLED WITH mixed emotions over what had happened with Gloria. He knew he'd handled the situation poorly, but what would his presence during her miscarriage have done? It wouldn't have saved his child and Gloria would have probably still hated him. And although he felt guilty about it, a part of him was relieved that he wouldn't have to ever explain to his wife what had happened. He knew that there was a chance that Gloria would still try and blow up his spot. She had to be pissed off about him having her things from the hotel room delivered to her and shipping her back home like she was cargo, but a lot of men wouldn't have done that much. She should be grateful.

Just to be safe, though, Ricardo decided to take out

some insurance. He didn't want to lose his wife; he loved her. She was always there for him and until recently she'd let him make whatever moves he wanted without so much as a word in opposition. He wanted things back the way they were and he knew exactly how to make that happen.

"Heaven, baby, I want to talk to you about something," Rico said to his wife upon his return from Miami.

"What is it?" she asked.

"I want you to know that I've been doing a lot of thinking lately. I've heard the things that you've been saying to me, about not spending enough time with you. And you know what? You're right. I haven't been around enough. But that's going to change starting with this day forward. I want you to be my partner in every way, baby. It was wrong of me to leave you here from day to day waiting around for me. I hope that you will come to work at the dealership with me. We're growing so much and I want you to know everything so that if anything ever happens to me, you'll be able to keep Diaz Brothers Import Auto afloat."

"If anything ever happens to you? Honey, please don't talk like that," Heaven said.

"I'm just being realistic. Nothing in this life is guaranteed, not even our next breath. When a man comes to grips with that, it changes him. I've been thinking about my life before you and my life with you and I know that the one thing I can be sure of in life that I'll never regret is having married you."

"Oh Rico," Heaven said with a smile on her face and tears in her eyes.

"And the only thing that can make being married to you any better is if the two of us start a family together."

"A family? Like a baby?" Heaven asked.

"Yes, like a baby. What do you say?" Rico knew that Heaven's family values would prevail over her anger if she ever found out about his affair with Gloria and the pregnancy. She'd never leave him if she was the mother of his child, and he'd have her right where he wanted her and needed her, by his side.

"Oh baby, I say yes." Heaven threw her arms around her husband's neck and squeezed him tight.

Rico scooped up Heaven in his arms and led her to the bedroom. He lay her down gently on the bed and slowly removed her clothes, kissing the exposed skin as he took off each article. Heaven shivered as Rico's mouth explored her body hungrily, bringing her to climax after climax. By the time he entered her, Heaven felt as though she had no energy left, but she willed herself to move in harmony with him.

"I love you," Ricardo told her over and over, and after he climaxed he lay there on top of her, kissing her and telling her all the things he knew she wanted and needed to hear.

"I hope I got pregnant," Heaven said.

"If you're not, we're going to have fun trying," Rico told her.

Heaven snuggled next to her husband. She was happier than she'd been in a long time but she still had nagging doubts. What had happened in Miami that had made him want to change so drastically? She wasn't sure what it was, but she hoped that her prayers had finally been answered. Just in case, she thanked God, making sure to apologize for her lack of faith.

Chapter 14
THE MiSSiON

GLORIA CRUZ WAS A woman who had one foot in the streets and the other in the world of dance. She'd been a natural at all forms of dance, from salsa to ballet, and luckily for her, her talent had been nurtured by her mother, who'd made sure her daughter had the best lessons that money could buy. Gloria's talent had enabled her to travel all over the world, giving her a sophisticated demeanor, but Gloria was hood through and through. Her ear was always planted firmly to the streets; she knew who all the major players were and what moves they were making. She had felt that it was her right to know what went on in her man's world, and she wanted to be the first to know if he started seeing someone else, but now that things were decidedly different between her and Rico, her street knowledge was going to serve a far more nefarious purpose.

Gloria sent Rico a few texts from the hospital, letting him know where she was and what happened, but she got no reply. All she got was her bags, a first-class airline ticket back to Chicago, and an envelope with five thousand dollars in it delivered to her by one of the Diaz do-boys. Gloria was livid. Did that bastard think that was all she was worth? A measly fucking five stacks! Well, she had something for his ass. She was going to destroy Ricardo Diaz, even if it took her the rest of her life.

DRESSED TO KILL, GLORIA hopped in her BMW M3 and headed south from her downtown apartment. She was a woman on a mission. She got on the Dan Ryan Expressway and headed south until she connected to the Indiana Toll Road. She paid the toll and drove another twenty minutes until she reached the Broadway exit. She was in the heart of Gary, Indiana.

Gloria hooked a left and drove until she approached a baseball stadium connected to a Bennigan's. She pulled into the Bennigan's parking lot and drove until she saw a lighted neon sign that read THE DIAMOND CENTER. The Diamond Center was one of Gary's hottest nightspots. For the twenty-something crowd, it was pretty much the *only* nightspot. There were cars galore cruising the lot, and a line formed outside the door.

Knowing that she was on foreign soil, Gloria did something she never did under ordinary circumstances. She stood at the back of the line. She didn't want to piss anyone off before she'd accomplished her goal. The line moved quickly, and Gloria paid her twenty-dollar entry to the pretty woman behind the counter who everyone called Mom, also known as Miss Carmen. Her son Big Pooch was the owner of the Bennigan's and the nightclub and Miss Carmen kept a watchful eye on her son's budding business.

Gloria made her way to the bar and ordered a Courvoisier on the rocks. She scanned the crowd, keeping an eye out for ballers. She took in what everyone was wearing from head to toe, and made note of the men that the women seemed to be paying the most attention to. In particular, she kept her eye on a girl who seemed to know everybody. She flitted about the club, speaking to everyone who seemed to be anyone. She also drank a lot. Gloria kept her post for an hour or so until she saw the girl stagger to the bathroom. She followed the girl inside the restroom.

"Woo, it's hot out there," Gloria said, fanning herself as the two of them waited for an available stall.

"I know that's right," the girl slurred. She looked at Gloria curiously. "You ain't from Gary, are you?" she asked.

"Nah, I'm from the Chi. I just heard that it's poppin' over here so I decided to check it out. My girls are supposed to be meeting me, but I think they must have gotten lost," Gloria lied.

"Where you live in Chicago?" the girl asked.

"Downtown," Gloria said.

"For real? Why come here?" The girl gave Gloria a puzzled look.

"My girl Chanté said her friend Black be chilling up here," Gloria said. "I don't know him, though. She said he's real good people. He's supposed to be major." Gloria smiled at the girl as if they were best friends.

"If she's talking about the Black I know, he ain't that good," the girl said. Jackpot! Gloria knew she'd hit paydirt.

"He hangs out with some crew called the G.I. Boys, right?" Gloria asked nonchalantly. The girl's expression changed.

"Look, honey, I don't know who this Chanté chick is, and frankly I don't know who you are. But you don't know Black and you ain't looking for him unless you're looking for trouble," the girl said.

"I'm not looking for no trouble," Gloria stated. "This is a *business* meeting," she continued carefully.

"Business?" the girl asked suspiciously.

"Yeah, business. And if you can tell me where I can find him, I'll make it worth your while."

"How much worth my while?" Drunk or not, the girl could smell money in the air.

"Let's say a couple of Benjamins."

"Are you serious?"

"Yes." Gloria pulled out two crisp hundred-dollar bills from her purse. She also had a switchblade in there beneath the lining in case anyone wanted to try her. The girl took the bills and pocketed them.

"Consider this your exit fee. I'm gonna take this money and let you leave here without getting your ass kicked," the girl said with a cruel laugh.

"What?" Gloria asked, shocked.

"You heard me. Take your ass back to Chicago where you belong before you get hurt," the girl said with a sneer.

Gloria was tempted to pull out her blade and buck-fifty the bitch, but knew that although she and the drunk girl were the only two people waiting in the restroom, she could be seriously outnumbered in less than a minute.

"You have a nice night," Gloria said, walking with haste out of the restroom, realizing that she'd have to find Black another way.

HEAVEN'S FURY

• • •

GLORIA HIT UP EVERY club and lounge in Gary in search of Black, although she performed her search in a more discreet fashion. It was a feat that only took a couple of hours, but she still came up empty-handed. Frustrated, she pulled into a gas station to fill up her car before she headed home. A crackhead approached her the instant she got out of her car.

"I'm not in the mood and I don't have any money," Gloria warned him.

"Come on. I know a high-class broad like you can spare some change," the crackhead pleaded.

"Broad?" Gloria's head snapped back, then she laughed. She wasn't about to waste her time cussing out a drug-addicted panhandler. She went inside and paid for her gas and then returned to her whip to pump it. The crackhead had already removed the nozzle from the pump and was trying to pry open her gas tank.

"Hey!" she shouted. "Cut that shit out!"

"I'm just trying to help, pretty lady."

"Thanks but no thanks," she said. "The tank has a release button on the *inside* of the car."

"Okay, so release it and I'll pump your gas."

"Just leave, okay?" Gloria insisted.

"I'm trying to help, that's all."

"I don't need your help," Gloria replied.

"Suit yourself," the crackhead said, handing her the nozzle. "What you doing over here anyway?"

"Looking for someone," Gloria said curtly.

"Did you find him?" the crackhead asked.

"No, I didn't," she said. "Wait, why am I still talking to you?" Gloria shook her head. It was definitely time to go home.

"'Cuz I'm handsome?" the crackhead asked, revealing a toothless grin. That made Gloria laugh.

"I knew it. I knew I could make you smile. Now, how's about a dollar?" The crackhead began to dance a little jig in front of her.

"If you really wanted to make me smile, you'd tell me how to find who I'm looking for."

"Who is it?" the crackhead asked.

"I seriously doubt you can help me," Gloria said.

"Don't hurt to ask," the crackhead replied.

"Fine, I'm looking for a guy called Black."

"I know a couple of Blacks," the crackhead told Gloria. Gloria thought about things. Who better to help her find a drug dealer than a drug addict? Gloria grinned.

"Well, the one I'm looking for is a hustler. A big-time one. You know him?"

"Shee-it! Who don't know that crazy motherfucker? He's a stone killer. What you want with him?"

"Don't worry about that. Tell me where I can find him and I'll make it worth your while."

The crackhead's eyes roamed over Gloria's curves. Gloria pursed her lips in disgust.

"I meant that I'd make it worth your while *this* way." She pulled a twenty-dollar bill out of her purse and handed it to him.

"Cool with me," the crackhead said. "You ain't my type no way. I like sisters."

"Well, bully for you. Now, do you know where I can find him?"

"He hangs out at the pool hall across the street from Bennigan's a lot. If he ain't there, he's at his house."

"You know where he lives?" Gloria asked.

"Yeah. We went to school together. I've known him my whole life. Shee-it. He the one that used to serve me back in the day. He the one who got me hooked."

Gloria didn't give a fuck. She handed the addict a piece of paper and a pen.

"Write down his address," she told him. She hoped she wouldn't have to approach Black at home, but she was willing to if it would help her accomplish her mission. Gloria gave the crackhead another twenty and sped off toward the pool hall.

• • •

GLORIA WALKED IN AND coughed on the thick layer of smoke that blanketed the pool hall. It was tastefully decorated and had a bar, tables and chairs, and a dartboard. Gloria sidled up to the bar and ordered a Courvoisier and slid the bartender a fifty-dollar bill.

"I'm looking for a man named Black," she said with a wink. Gloria made sure to stick her chest out so the bartender got an eyeful of her cleavage. "I'd sure appreciate it if you could help me find him."

"He's in the corner in the back," the bartender said. Gloria looked toward the back of the pool hall. There was a man seated at a table and two men posted on either side of him. They looked like they weren't to be fucked with.

"Thanks," Gloria said, trying to mask her nervousness.

The bartender took the bill and let his fingers glide over Gloria's hand. "But are you sure you're looking for him? I'm a much nicer man."

"I'm sure," Gloria said, taking her hand off the bar. She sashayed to the back and caught the eye of every man in the pool hall. Gloria had a killer stroll, one that could make a blind man see and resurrect the dead with her ass of life switching to and fro. Rico once told her that she walked like her pussy was good. She became more determined at the thought of Rico and hardened her gaze. She wanted Black to know she was about business and wouldn't be intimidated, even though the men posted on either side of him looked like they were ready to kill her with their bare hands if need be.

Black lit a cigarillo as he watched the sexy Latina *mami* walk toward him. He took in her curves and her serious expression and was intrigued. She stood before him and licked her lips.

"Black?" she asked.

"Who wants to know?" Black replied.

"I want to know," Gloria told him.

"And just who are you?"

"I'm a friend."

"A friend?" asked one of the bodyguards.

"Yes, I believe that he'll see me as a friend once he realizes that I'm a woman with some very valuable information for him."

Black blew a ring of smoke into the air. "Sit down," he said. Gloria sat down. "What kind of information do you have for me, and what is it going to cost me?"

"This info isn't going to cost you a thing, but it's going to make you millions. You and I have an enemy in common," Gloria stated. "I believe we both want the same thing, to see him fall. Not just a little, but utterly and completely."

"And who would this enemy be?" Black asked Gloria. She smiled at him and he smiled back, although his smile was much more like a sneer.

"A certain exotic car dealer in Chicago," Gloria told Black. Black reached for his piece. Gloria peeped his action and spoke quickly.

"I know this sounds crazy and it looks suspect, me coming in here out of nowhere. I know about the shit that's been going down and frankly, I'm surprised that I even found you."

Black laughed.

"What? Did you think I'd be in hiding or something? I hold this city down. Them pussy boys don't scare me. They already tried once to get at me and failed. They got a death wish if they come for me again," Black said. "But you know what makes more sense? It makes more sense that the Diaz brothers would send a pretty woman like you over here to distract me than for you to come over here all by yourself looking for revenge." Black pulled his pistol from his waistband and set it on the table. He aimed the barrel at Gloria. "You do realize it would be nothing for me to pull the trigger and blow your brains out, don't you?" he asked menacingly.

Gloria swallowed hard. Her throat was dry and her voice was scratchy when she replied. "I can see that. But I'm willing to take that chance," she said. "I can guarantee you that I'm not here to cause you any harm or set you up." Gloria thought to herself that maybe coming to Gary wasn't such a good idea. She'd allowed her anger and thirst for vengeance to propel her into enemy territory. Who knew what would happen to her?

"Just what did Diaz do to you to make you want to see him fall so bad?"

"He killed my kid," Gloria said. "And I believe in an eye for an eye."

Chapter 15
FRiENDS AND FOES

HEAVEN WAS AWAKENED AROUND midnight by her cell phone. Rico was late, but he had called earlier and swore that he would come home and that he wouldn't be too much longer.

"Hello?" Heaven rubbed her eyes and sat up in bed.

"Hello, Heaven, is that you?" It was Gloria. They'd spoken on the phone practically every day over the past week, chatting for hours on end. They'd even gone to lunch a couple of times and Heaven was starting to feel close to Gloria.

"Yeah, Glory?" Heaven asked.

"Yeah, it's me," she said.

"What's going on?"

Gloria began to cry softly on the other end.

"I'm sorry to burden you with my troubles. I really hate to be calling you like this, I mean, I don't want to be a bother, but there's really no one else for me to call." Gloria sniffled over the telephone. She was laying on the heavy theatrics for the performance of a lifetime.

"Glory, there's no reason to apologize. That's what friends are for." Gloria couldn't believe how naïve and trusting Heaven was. There was no way that she would ever consider someone a friend that she had just met, even if they did talk on the phone and grabbed lunch together.

"You're so sweet, Heaven."

"Hey, it's nothing. Women have to stick together," Heaven said. "But tell me, what's the matter?"

"I need someone to talk to," Gloria said. "It's about my pregnancy."

"I'll talk to you," Heaven said. Chatting would help the time pass until Rico got home. "Whatever's on your mind you can tell me."

"I-I don't want to talk about it over the phone," Gloria said. "And I don't want to be alone."

"Do you want to come over here?" Heaven offered. "Or I can come over there," she suggested.

"Isn't your husband going to get mad?" Gloria asked, but she knew that Rico wasn't home. Her sources had assured her that he was still at the auto dealership.

"Well, my husband isn't here right now."

"If you tell me where you live I can come over there. I'd hate for your husband to come home and you not be there. That would be hard to explain."

"I guess you're right about that. So come on over." Heaven gave Gloria her address and then threw on a terry-cloth sweatsuit. She called Rico on his cell phone to see where he was and to let him know that she was going to have a guest, but he didn't answer. She called him at the dealership and he didn't answer there, either. Heaven sighed and wondered if her husband had reverted back to his old ways, then she went downstairs to wait for Gloria.

Twenty minutes later, Heaven's doorbell rang. She peered out the curtains in the living room and saw a cherry red M3 parked in her driveway and Gloria standing on her doorstep. She opened the door to her home and welcomed Gloria inside.

"Can I get you something? Some water or juice?" Heaven offered.

"How about a Grey Goose and cranberry?" Gloria asked.

"Wow, you must really be stressing to want to drink

while you're pregnant. Why don't you sit down and tell me what's going on with you."

"Well, for starters, I'm not pregnant anymore," Gloria told Heaven.

"What happened?" Heaven asked with concern. Gloria turned on the waterworks.

"Oh Heaven, it's such a long story," Gloria said.

"Don't worry. We've got all night," Heaven said.

HYCKEF PULLED HIS WHITE Maserati into the gas station on State Street and Roosevelt Road, not far from his post at the Ickes Homes. A bum in a grungy baseball cap, dirty wife-beater, filthy khakis, and sandals walked up to his ride with a handful of rags and attempted to clean the windows.

"I'm good, man," Hyckef said. The man continued to wipe and rub, smearing dirt all over the windshield. "I said I'm good, man," Hyckef repeated with more bass in his voice. The man kept dirtying up the windshield. Hyckef got out of the car and walked aggressively toward the man. The man sneered at Hyckef, then pulled out a Luger with a silencer on the end. Hyckef's eyes registered shock when he realized the identity of the windshield washer. It was Black.

Black popped one shot into Hyckef's gut and shoved him into the car. Black pushed Hyckef's long legs into the passenger's side, then he got in after him. Black gunned the engine and rode to the White Castle a few blocks away. His crew awaited him there in a dark blue cargo van. The crew moved Hyckef's bleeding body into the van and went to work on him, literally pouring salt into his wound.

Black knew that Hyckef wasn't the hard-core thug he made himself out to be. He figured that he'd roll over on his partners quickly and he was right. Within ten minutes, the crew had tortured Hyckef into revealing what apartment in the Ickes the stash of drugs was in, where the money was, and the combination to the safe where it was all located. Hyckef was clinging to life but begging for death. It would come soon enough. Black and his crew proceeded to the Ickes.

KINO AND YSETTE DIAZ slumbered peacefully in their bed. They'd spent the evening making love and they were both exhausted. Outside two men, one tall and lanky and the other short and portly, both dressed in all black, worked quickly and stealthily. The tall man served as a lookout, crouched down in the bushes, while the short one disconnected the security system. When the burgular alarm was disarmed, the short man gave his partner a hand signal and then went around to the back of the house. He pulled out a special jump key that had been filed down to certain specifications and stuck it in the dead bolt. Then he took a hammer and tapped it a few times. With ease, he was able to unlock the door and he opened it and went inside.

At the same time, his partner went to the front of the house and used the same technique to enter the home. The man who had entered from the front went directly upstairs, a semiautomatic pistol ready to blow the head off anything that moved. The man who entered from the back did a sweep of the bottom level of the house. It was all clear. He met his partner on the second level of the house. They went from bedroom to bedroom until they found the one they were looking for.

Like vultures, they descended on the sleeping and unsuspecting couple. Each man placed a hand over the mouths of Kino and Ysette. Startled, each of them opened their eyes only to be staring down the barrel of a gun. Tears automatically streamed down Ysette's face. Without hesitation or mercy, the man holding the gun to Ysette squeezed the trigger and fired a solitary bullet into her skull.

"Say one word and you're next," the short gunman said to Kino.

"I don't give a fuck," Kino replied. "You killed my wife. You better kill me now because if you don't, I'm going to slowly torture each of you."

"You and what army?" the tall gunman asked with a

laugh. "Your boy Hyckef is probably floating in Lake Michigan right about now."

"Yeah, man," said the short one. "And your brother and his wife are about to meet their makers, too."

Kino glared at the men who were standing in front of him. He knew he had to make a move, a bold and crazy one that might end up costing him his life, but what difference did that make? His wife was dead, killed right before his eyes, and the men who were holding him at gunpoint had already let him know that they intended on leaving no survivors.

"What do you want from me?" Kino asked.

"Some information," the short gunman said.

"Where's the money and the dope?" the tall one asked.

"I keep my money in the bank," Kino said. "I may have a few grand in the house, but that's it."

"Bullshit!" the tall one said.

"No, it's the truth. I'm a legitimate businessman. Where else would I keep my money?"

"What about the money you make on the side? The money you don't want Uncle Sam to know about?" the gunman demanded.

"It's in a bank in Panama," Kino said and he was telling the truth. At the same time, he reached under his pillow and pulled out the Saturday-night special he kept hidden there for precisely these types of situations. There was plenty of heat in the house, but there was no way that he was going to be able to reach it without taking out at least one of his adversaries. Kino squeezed two shots in rapid succession, attempting to maim his captors, but it didn't make a difference. The gunmen were rocking Teflon vests under their hoodies and were totally unfazed by the shots. Kino should have aimed for the head.

"Fuck," Kino muttered as a red beam shone in his face and a gun went off.

At Diaz Brothers Import Auto, Ricardo was busy working on a spreadsheet. He looked at the clock on the wall of his office. It read 2:45 a.m. Rico decided to call it a night. He'd promised Heaven that he would cut down on his hours; he didn't want her to get upset with him again. He picked up the phone to call his wife.

"Hey babe," she said when she answered.

"Hey. What are you doing awake? It's almost three a.m."

"Well, my friend called me needing to talk a little while ago. She came over."

"What friend?" Rico asked. Heaven didn't hang out with anyone besides Ysette and the occasional chick from her old neighborhood.

"Well, she's a new friend. Gloria Cruz," Heaven explained. "We met a few weeks ago." Rico almost fainted when Heaven told him her new friend's name.

"Heaven, can I use your bathroom?" Gloria asked Heaven.

"Sure, there's one down the hall on your right," Heaven said. Gloria grabbed her purse and retreated to the restroom and Heaven returned to her phone call.

"I hope you don't mind me having company so late, but she lost her baby," Heaven whispered. "She's in a really bad way right now and she didn't want to be alone."

"I see," he said with a little cough. "I'm on the way home now," he told her.

"Okay, babe, I'll see you soon," Heaven said.

Rico had no idea what Gloria was up to, but he was damn sure about to find out. He sent her a text:

What the fuck are you doing in my house? I'm on the way home and your ass better be gone when I get there.

He waited for a moment for her to respond. His cell phone vibrated and he answered it without even checking the caller ID.

"Yeah," he said angrily.

"Your boy Hyckef is dead. Your brother and sister-in-law

are dead. You're next," a deep and gravelly voice boomed menacingly on the other end.

Rico's knees buckled. This had to be a joke. His brother, his best friend, and his brother's wife couldn't all be dead.

"Who is this?" he barked.

"This is your worst fucking nightmare," Black said.

"Is this that black-ass motherfucker from G.I.?" Rico asked.

"Your black ass is one to talk, Ricardo. Don't let that curly hair on your head get you twisted, pretty boy."

"Your ass is dead," Rico spat venomously.

"No, your wife is the dead one. I'm on my way to your house right now and I just might have to tap that fat ass of hers before I kill her," Black threatened.

"Leave my wife out of this," Rico said.

"Your wife is already in it. I've got a friend over there right now who's going to let me walk right in the front door. As soon as I'm in, wifey is a dead woman. That is, unless you cooperate." Black was lying through his teeth. He had absolutely no intention on leaving anyone in that house alive when he was done, not even Gloria. He couldn't trust a bitch that would set up her own man. The only way that he could ensure that Gloria wouldn't turn on him was to eliminate her. He was using the threat for leverage. If Rico knew that everyone was a dead man, he'd attempt to go out like a soldier. Black needed Rico alive in order to get information. Black planned on forcing Rico's hand to gain access to his safe, his autos, his bank account information, and his stash of product. Then he'd take him out.

Rico thought about what Black said. He couldn't believe his ears. Gloria had been working with the enemy to set him up *and* had insinuated herself into his wife's life somehow. He never would have dreamed in a million years that things would turn out this way.

"What the fuck do you want?" Rico asked, agitated.

"Simply put, I want everything that you have. I'm taking over your South Side territory," Black told him.

"Take it. I want out of the dope biz anyway. Just leave my wife alone!"

Black laughed and hung up the phone.

GLORIA SHUT THE BATHROOM door behind her and locked it. She knew that no one would come inside, but she wasn't going to take any chances. Gloria's hands shook as she keyed in a text message to Black:

My cover is blown. Rico knows that I'm here.

She hoped that little unexpected occurrence didn't create a snag in the plan. Ricardo Diaz was a dead man, even if that meant that she had to kill him herself.

Gloria put her cell phone away and flushed the toilet. Then she ran the water in the sink as if she were washing her hands. She caught a glimpse of herself in the mirror and felt a twinge of guilt. What she was doing was dirty as hell, but *someone* had to pay for the death of her child and all the pain that she'd gone through. Heaven was a sweetheart and it was too bad that she was going to have to go down with the ship, but that wasn't Gloria's concern. Heaven should have known the danger involved when she married a man like Rico.

Gloria returned to the living room where Heaven sat.

"Everything all right?" Heaven asked her.

"Yeah, I guess. It's just that this is so hard for me."

"Why don't you tell me what happened. My *abuela* always said that confession is good for the soul."

Heaven sat transfixed as Gloria regaled her with the tale of her no-account ex-boyfriend who'd left her alone during her time of need.

"He left me on the hotel floor to die." Gloria sniffed. "I told him that something was wrong with the baby, but that didn't matter to him."

"That's so awful," Heaven said sympathetically. "I can't believe that happened to you. I wish there was something that I could do."

"Just listening has done more for me than you'll ever know," Gloria said with a smile.

"What made your guy flip the script the way that he did? I would think that any man would be happy to have a baby with you."

"He's married," Gloria confessed.

"Really," Heaven replied. "How could you allow yourself to get mixed up with a creep like that?" Heaven asked.

"I've known him forever," Gloria said. "I went away to study and he felt that he couldn't wait for me. He married someone else, but that was a mistake. We never stopped loving each other and reconnected. At least I thought that we never stopped loving each other. Obviously, he never really loved me at all."

"Don't sweat it, Glory. One day you'll meet your Prince Charming and he won't be married. He'll treat you with the love and respect that you deserve, you'll see. Just trust in the Lord. He can turn anything around." Heaven was interrupted by the sound of her phone vibrating. She looked down at the caller ID display. It was Rico calling again. What could he want? "Excuse me just a second, Glory," Heaven said.

"What's up, babe?" she asked.

"Go into a private room. Now!" Rico ordered. "I need to tell you something very important."

"What's going on?"

"Just do as I say," Rico ordered.

"I'll be right back, Glory," Heaven said, and went into the kitchen.

"What's with you?" Heaven asked Rico when she was out of earshot.

"Heaven, baby, listen carefully. Your life is in danger," Rico said, speaking a mile a minute.

"What? Rico, you've got to slow down. What are you talking about?"

"Baby, I don't have time to explain things, but you've got to get out of the house!"

"Rico, you're scaring me."

"I'm sorry. But this is some serious shit, all right? Get out of the house *now!*" Rico yelled.

"You need to tell me what's going on!"

"What's going on is that I really fucked up and I don't know if you'll ever forgive me," Rico told her. "But you've got to trust me now if you never have before."

"I trust you," Heaven said. "Now, tell me what's going on!"

"Fine and after I do, get out. You promise?" Rico begged.

"I promise."

"I don't have time for a lengthy explanation, but that woman, your so-called friend Gloria, she isn't who she claims to be. She was my girlfriend a long time ago. I think she's in on a plot to kill me."

"Kill you? Why would anyone want to kill you? Wait a minute! Are you the one that got her pregnant?" Heaven shrieked.

"Calm down!" Rico demanded. "I don't want her to hear you."

"Let me tell you something, Ricardo Diaz. Gloria Cruz is the last person you should be worried about right now. Answer the fucking question!"

"Yes, but—"

"But, my ass. You mean to tell me that the woman sitting in my living room right now is one of your ready-made whores?"

"It wasn't like that. Trust me, baby, she doesn't mean anything to me."

"Shut up!" Heaven screamed.

"Baby, listen. You've got to get out of the house right now. Hyckef, Kino, and Ysette have all been killed. The next target is you," Rico said, but he said it to the dial tone. Heaven had already hung up the phone.

Chapter 16
HELL HATH NO FURY

RICO SPED TO HIS home, hoping that he would make it there before Black did. He had no idea what he would do once he got there. He had a gun, but he also had a feeling that he was going to have to go up against an army. What if it was already too late? What if Gloria planned on hurting Heaven? He would kill her with his bare hands if she laid a hand on his wife.

Rico's best friend, brother, and sister-in-law were all dead. He regretted not taking care of the situation with Black immediately, but there was no sense in crying over spilled milk, at least not at that moment. He'd have the rest of his life—if he lived—to think about everything he had done wrong. The main thing on his mind was saving his wife.

• • •

BLACK AND HIS SOLDIERS met up in the parking lot of the closed-down co-op grocery on Forty-seventh and Lake Park. All the other businesses were closed, so although they were on a relatively busy street, they were alone.

"Are y'all ready to do this?" Black asked his army. "It's takeover time." Black's troops responded positively. They were on ten, totally amped and bloodthirsty.

"Three men will take the back door. One man will stand on the east and west sides of the house. If either of you see so much as the whites of someone's eyes, blast. Don't hesitate. I don't care if it's a senior citizen or a toddler. Kill the motherfuckers. The only exceptions are Mr. and Mrs. Diaz. We're going to have a little fun with them first. The rest of you guys will come with me, right through the front door. Understood?"

"Understood," the men said in unison.

HEAVEN STOOD IN HER kitchen seething. She'd never been so angry in her entire life. She was dangerously angry, angry enough to kill. A piercing pain shot through Heaven's temples. Her vision blurred slightly and her breath came in quick, short gasps. Her throat felt dry so she poured a glass of water and gulped it down.

Heaven thought about the facts in front of her. Gloria was a total phony. She'd been using Heaven all along for her own sick pleasure. Ricardo was a liar and a cheat. He'd used her and taken her for granted for years, but that was all about to end. She'd been played for a fool for the very last time. It was time for her to stand up for herself, to stop being a damn doormat for everyone to trample over. She knew what she had to do.

Heaven walked calmly up the back stairs of her home and went into the master bedroom. She went into the his-and-hers walk-in closet and looked on the shelf where Rico kept his sweaters. She felt around for the gun she knew her husband kept there and when she found it, she checked to see if it was loaded. It was. She grabbed the extra clip that she found and then tucked the piece into her waistband and the ammo in her pocket and headed back downstairs.

"You scared me!" Gloria exclaimed when she saw Heaven, putting her hand over her heart. She had started to grow nervous when Rico called Heaven again. Gloria had no idea where Black was, but she wasn't going to stick around and wait. Something was wrong, Gloria felt it in her bones. She knew that Heaven had been tipped off. "I thought you were in the kitchen," Gloria said with a smile.

"I was," Heaven said blandly. "I needed to go upstairs to get something."

"Oh," Gloria replied, eyeing Heaven curiously. "Well, look, I can tell that now's not a good time. I've bent your ear with my sob stories for long enough. I'm gonna cut outta here."

"No, you're not going to go anywhere," Heaven told her. "I just got off the phone with my husband and he just informed me that you have been fucking him for our entire marriage."

Gloria looked like a deer caught in headlights.

"Don't tell me the cat's got your tongue. You had plenty to say when you were pretending to be my friend. You were bold enough to come to my house with your little bullshit story. Now you don't have any words?"

"Fuck it, then," Gloria said, full of bravado. Black would be there any second to handle shit. There was no need to play coy anymore. "Yeah, I pretended to be your friend."

"And that's not all you did, was it?" Heaven asked her.

"Nah, it wasn't. Your husband needs to pay for what he did to me. You're a nice girl, and it's too bad you're caught in the middle of all this, but Rico killed my child."

"Spare me, bitch! You're not the least bit sorry. You screwed my husband and you thought you were going to screw me, but the tables have turned."

"Who are you calling a bitch?" Gloria asked, full of sass, standing and putting her hands on her curvaceous hips.

156

"You're the only bitch in the room. I'm talking to you. Now sit your ass down," Heaven said, extracting the gun from her waistband.

"Oh shit," Gloria said under her breath.

"Oh shit is right. You're in deep now. You're in a world of shit."

"I don't think so. Even if you kill me, which I know you don't have the guts to do, someone will be here any minute to take care of you. Your husband's organization is crumbling as we speak. By now, your brother- and sister-in-law are dead. Once my boy Black gets ahold of Rico, it's a wrap for him, too," Gloria stated.

"I'm not going to kill you, at least not yet. Death is too good for you, bitch. I want you to suffer," Heaven said. "I want you to hurt the way that I hurt. I want you to feel the pain I felt when my husband was in your bed and I was up wondering where he was and what he was doing."

"Rico was mine first anyway. If anyone stole him it was you. It's not my fault that you don't know how to keep him happy."

Heaven laughed and pointed the gun at Gloria's thigh. She squeezed the trigger and her arm jerked at the recoil. Gloria howled in pain as blood began to ooze from her thigh.

"I'm not thinking about Ricardo or his happiness right

now. All I care about is revenge." Heaven aimed the gun at Gloria's knee cap and fired again. "Ooh, that looks like that hurt," she said softly.

Gloria screamed. The pain she was in was excruciating. Even if Heaven didn't kill her, from the looks of her injuries, Gloria would never walk again without a limp, let alone dance. Heaven walked over to the wet bar and poured herself a stiff drink, Rémy Martin on the rocks. She took a sip and felt the liquid burn her throat and chest. She took another sip and felt her courage and anger grow exponentially. Not being a heavy drinker, the potent cognac went to work almost immediately. Heaven walked back over to where Gloria was bleeding and crying.

"Why my husband? Why couldn't you find your own man? You knew he was married. What satisfaction did you get from being second best?"

"Fuck you," Gloria spat. "I didn't give a fuck about you or your marriage."

"And obviously, Rico didn't give a fuck about you. That's why he didn't want your bastard child, you slut." Heaven aimed the gun at Gloria's feet and blasted a shot in each one. She'd never heard such a bloodcurdling scream in her life as the one that Gloria let out. Heaven poured a bit of her cocktail into the bullet wound on Gloria's thigh.

"Oh my God!" Gloria shrieked.

"God? You want to call on Him now?" Heaven asked.

"You weren't thinking about God when you were screwing my husband, were you?"

"You're crazy!" Gloria uttered through her pain.

"You damn straight I'm crazy. Someone named Black is on his way here to kill me. My sister- and brother-in-law are dead. You've been fucking my husband, who just happens to be a notorious drug lord, and I've played the fool the whole time. I'd say that I have a right to be crazy." Heaven looked at Gloria lying maimed on the floor. She hated her with a passion she'd never felt for anyone.

"You know the police will be here any second," Gloria told Heaven. "I'm sure your neighbors heard gunshots and called the police."

"Oh, I doubt that," Heaven said. "The walls of this house are solid concrete. We've got double-paned storm windows. I can barely hear what's going on outside so I doubt the outside can hear what's going on inside."

"I need a doctor," Gloria begged. "Please."

"No, you're going to need a coroner. You won't leave my house alive."

"When Black and his crew get here they're going to shoot the shit out of you," Gloria said. She was growing weak from the loss of blood. "If you call an ambulance now we can both make it out of here. If you don't, we're both dead."

"I can make it out of here alive if I want to. I can walk

out the door, get in my car, and go right to the authorities. But you see, I don't really care if I live or die right now. I don't give a fuck about anything."

There was the sound of a key turning in the lock. Heaven and Gloria both looked up. Heaven aimed the gun at the door and waited for it to open. When it did, she didn't hesitate to squeeze off two shots. A body fell to the ground. It was Rico.

Chapter 17
UNFORGiVABLE

"Rico," Gloria whispered. She was growing weaker and weaker by the minute.

"Heaven!" Rico screamed. The wounds he'd suffered were superficial. He'd been hit in the leg and in the shoulder. He was in pain and somewhat immobilized, but he wouldn't die from the bullet wounds. He looked at Gloria's bleeding body sprawled out on the floor. "Baby, what have you done?" he asked, alarmed.

"I did what I had to do," Heaven said. "That bitch set me up. She pretended to be my friend and all the while she was fucking you. And not only that, you knocked her up and then had the nerve to come back home to me and try to make a baby with me."

"Heaven, I know I fucked up," Rico began.

"You damn straight you did. You fucked up big time. I would have done anything for you. I loved you with all my heart and soul, but that wasn't enough for you. You're a real asshole," Heaven told her husband.

"I am, baby. You're right about that. I regret it all. But right now we've got to get out of here."

"We aren't going anywhere," Heaven said.

"Look, there's a crew of motherfuckers on their way over here to kill us. We've got to get out of here right now!" Heaven looked at Rico and Gloria lying on the floor. She hated both of them.

"I don't care," Heaven told Rico.

"Yes, you do," Rico said. "You're just upset. We don't have time to go through all this right now. We've got to go!"

"Maybe that didn't come out right. I meant, *you're* not going anywhere." Heaven quickly reloaded with the spare clip and aimed the gun at Rico, shooting him in the gut.

"I loved you so much," she said as she crouched over his body.

"Heaven, please . . ." Rico reached his hand out to his wife. She hawked and spit in his face.

"Fuck you," she said. "Fuck you and your whore." Heaven debated whether or not to finish the job on her husband and his mistress or to let Black and his crew do what they wanted. Either way, they were both dead, which was just what she wanted. Thoughts of the years she'd spent with Ricardo flooded her mind as tears filled her eyes. She held the gun up to her husband's head and screamed in anguish.

"Heaven," Rico said, looking up at her. "You're going to kill me?" She didn't know what she was going to do but she figured she needed to do it soon.

"Heaven," Gloria whispered. "You can't do this. You've got to get help before it's too late."

Rico looked at Heaven with sincere regret. "Forgive me," he whispered.

"This shit is unforgivable," she replied.

Heaven's hand shook as she pointed the gun at her target and fired one final shot.

Chapter 18
STREET LEGEND

BLACK'S CREW ARRIVED AT the Diaz home, jumped out of the cargo vans they occupied, and took their assigned posts. With guns drawn, Black and his men ran up the front stairs and kicked the door. It flung open easily and they nearly fell inside; the door had been left unlocked. Black gasped at the carnage he saw on the living room floor. A woman lay on the floor in a pool of blood. Her entire face had been blown off and she was unrecognizable. Next to her lay his nemesis, Ricardo Diaz, bleeding and gasping for breath. He was clearly on the brink of death.

What the fuck happened here? Black thought. He rushed to Rico's body.

"I need the combination to the safe," Black ordered.

Rico looked up at Black and said nothing.

"Come on, motherfucker!" Black shouted in frustration. "Tell me!"

The sound of sirens roared faintly in the distance.

"You hear that?" one of Black's henchmen asked. "We've gotta go!"

"Fuck that! I want what I came here for!" Black snarled.

"Man, we're all gonna get pinched if we don't haul ass."

"Then I'm gonna go out in a blaze of glory!" Black told him.

"Come on! Don't be crazy. We got what we wanted. This motherfucker is about to take an eternal dirt nap. The territory is yours."

"Yeah, but is this Rico's wife or that woman Gloria?" Black asked. "Her fucking face is blown off."

"Does it matter?" his crony asked.

"Yeah, it does. That bitch Gloria knows everything. She can't just go free. And if that's her and Rico's wife is gone, we gotta go find her and murk her ass."

"Then ask the motherfucker," Black's boy suggested.

"Who is this?" Black asked Rico, pointing the gun to his head. He knew his life was over regardless of what he said and it was because of his wife. But he knew what he had to say.

"It's my wife," Rico lied. He'd already caused Heaven enough pain. She deserved her freedom; she deserved to be safe. He owed her that. He just hoped that Heaven did what he was counting on her to do: live a quiet life without him and not draw any attention to herself. She was a smart woman, even if she had been blinded by love and trust. He knew that she would figure out a way to take care of herself. Hopefully, Black would let things die. But as Ricardo Diaz took his last breaths, he knew in his heart that a cold-hearted man like Black wouldn't be satisfied until he got what he wanted, which was everything that Heaven was entitled to as his widow. He'd find a way to complete his plan.

Black heard the sound of the sirens getting closer. He stood and pointed his gun at Rico. Rico looked at him with courage and strength; he wasn't afraid to die. His only regret was that he hadn't been a better husband. If he hadn't hooked up with Gloria, none of this would be happening to him, at least not the way that it had gone down. Black would have had to work a lot harder to take over Rico's empire.

Black pulled the trigger and ended Rico's life before heading out the door. His crew followed suit and piled back into the vans and disappeared into the night. As they drove back to Gary, Black thought about what he'd been able to get from the Diaz brothers. He'd robbed Rico and Kino for over a couple million in product and a few hundred thou in cash. He didn't have everything they'd owned; there was still the matter of several exotic cars that Black would probably never be able to get his hands on. But he'd achieved his goal. Not only was he the king of the Gary drug trade, but he'd expanded his territory into Chicago. No one before him had been able to successfully make that kind of move. Not only was he a very rich man, he was now a street legend.

Epilogue

HEAVEN HAD DRIVEN OUT of her garage just as Black and his crew stormed her home. If she had waited any longer she would have surely been killed. She had no idea where she was going or what to do next; it was like she was moving on autopilot. She thought about Ricardo's life insurance, the business, and the properties her late husband owned. It was all hers now. No longer would she have to sit and wait for Ricardo to come home. No longer would she have to wonder what she was doing wrong. She now saw that her solitude had never been her fault; her husband had been a self-centered, self-serving bastard who wouldn't have known what honesty and integrity were if they were tattooed on his forehead.

The sun was beginning to rise over Lake Michigan as she drove north on Lake Shore Drive. It symbolized to Heaven that no matter what happened in this world, life went on. The sun would rise, the sun would set, and although the cast of players changed daily, the drama of life never ended.

Heaven knew that she'd eventually have to go to the authorities. She also knew that they'd never be able to prove nor would the authorities even suspect that she'd killed her husband and his mistress, so she wasn't worried about that. If what had been said was true, there were several dead bodies linked to some man named Black, some man who might come after her to finish what he had started. That was what scared her. But Heaven knew that she was fortunate enough to have the money and resources to start her life all over again. It would be easy for her to disappear and to relocate her family. Flying under the radar would not be a problem. And Heaven knew that she had God on her side. At least she would after she did one final thing.

Heaven exited Lake Shore Drive and headed west until she was in her old neighborhood, Logan Square. She drove until she was in front of the church she'd grown up in, St. Michael the Archangel. She knew the door would be open. It was always open. She walked into the church and crossed herself and then ducked into a confessional. The priest made the sign of the cross and Heaven made it with him. She pulled out her old rosary, the one she had thrown in the gutter, and kissed it.

"Go on, my child," the priest said.

"In the name of the Father and of the Son and of the Holy Spirit. Forgive me, Father, for I have sinned . . ."

Turn the page for

G-UNiT BOOKS

excerpts of more
BY 50 CENT

DERELICT

By 50 Cent and Relentless Aaron

**DERELICT: Shamefully negligent in not
having done what one should have done.**

Prison: One of the few places on Earth where sharks sleep,
and where *"You reap what you sow."*

The note that Prisoner Jamel Ross attached,
with his so called "urgent request," to see the prison psychotherapist was supposed to appear desperate: *"I need to address some
serious issues because all I can think about is killing two people
when I leave here. Can you help me!"* And that's all he wrote. But
even more than the anger, revenge, and redemption Jamel was
ready to bring back to the streets, he also had the prison's psych
as a target; a target of his lust. And that was a more pressing issue
at the moment.

"As far back as I can remember life has been about growing pains,"
he told her. "I've been through the phases of a liar in my adoles-
cence, a hustler and thug in my teens, and an all-out con man in
my twenties. Maybe it was just my instincts to acquire what I considered resources—by whatever means necessary, but it's a shame
that once you get away with all of those behaviors, you become

good at it, like some twisted type of talent or profession. Eventually even lies feel like the truth . . .

". . . I had a good thing going with *Superstar*. The magazine. The cable television show. Meeting and comingling with the big-name celebrities and all. I was positioned to have the biggest multimedia company in New York; the biggest to focus on black entertainment exclusively. BET was based in Washington at the time, so I had virtually no competition. Jamel Ross, the big fish in a little pond . . .

"And of course I got away with murder, figuratively, when Angel—yes, the singer with the TV show and all her millions of fans—didn't go along with the authorities, including her mother, who wanted to hit me with child molestation, kidnapping, and other charges. I was probably dead wrong for laying with that girl before she turned eighteen. But Angel was a very grown-up seventeen-year-old. Besides, when I hit it she was only a few months shy from legal. So, gimme a break.

"In a strange way, fate came back to get my ass for all of my misdeeds. All of my pimp-mania. That cable company up in Connecticut (with more than four hundred stations and fifty-five million subscribers across the country) was purchased by an even larger entity. It turned my life around when that happened; made my brand-new, million-dollar contract null and void. There was no way that I could sue anyone because lawyers' fees are incredible and my company overextended itself with the big celebrations, the lavish spending, and the increased staff; my living expenses, including the midtown penthouse, and the car notes, and maintenance for Deadra and JoJo—my two lovers, at the time—were in excess of eleven thousand a month. Add that to the overhead at *Superstar* and, without a steady stream of cash flowing, I had an ever-growing monster on my hands.

"One other thing, both Deadra and JoJo became pregnant, so now I would soon have four who depended on me as the sole provider. Funny, all of this wasn't an issue when things were lean. When the sex was good and everyone was kissing my ass. Now, I'm the bad guy because the company's about to go belly-up."

With a little more than two years left to his eighty-four-month stretch, Jamel Ross finally got his wish, to sit and spill his guts to Dr. Kay Edmonson, the psychotherapist at Fort Dix—the Federal Correctional Institution that was a fenced-in forty-acre plot on the much bigger Fort Dix Army Base. Fort Dix was where Army reservists went to train, and simultaneously where felons did hard time for crimes gone wrong. With so many unused acres belonging to the government during peacetime, someone imagined that perhaps a military academy or some other type of income-producing entity would work on Fort Dix as well. So they put a prison there.

The way that Fort Dix was set up was very play it by ear. It was a growing project where new rules were implemented along the way. Sure, there was a Bureau of Prisons guidebook with regulations for both staff and convicts to follow. However, that BOP guidebook was very boilerplate, and it left the prison administrators in a position in which they had to learn to cope and control some three thousand offenders inside of the fences of what was the largest Federal population in the system. It was amazing how it all stayed intact for so long.

"On the pound" nicknames were appreciated and accepted since it was a step away from a man's birth name, or "government name," which was the name that all the corrections officers, administrative staff, and of course the courts, used when addressing convicts. So, on paper Jamel's name was Jamel Ross. On paper, Jamel Ross was not considered to be a person, but a "convict" with the registration number 40949–054, something like the forty thousandth prisoner to be filtered through the Southern District of New York. The "054" being the sort of area code in his prison ID number. He was sentenced by Judge Benison in October of 1997, committed to eighty-four months—no parole, and three years' probation. The conviction was for bank robbery. However, on appeal, the conviction was "adjusted" since there was no conclusive evidence that Jamel had a weapon. Nevertheless, Jamel certainly *did* have a weapon and fully intended to pull off a robbery, with a pen as his weapon. So, the time he was doing was more deserved than not.

But regardless of Jamel's level of involvement, it was suddenly very easy for him to share himself since he felt he had nothing to lose. It was much easier to speak to a reasonably attractive woman, as if there was good reasoning for the things he did and why. So, he went on explaining all of his dirty deeds to "Dr. Kay" Edmondson, as if this were a confessional where he'd be forgiven for his sins. And why not? She was a good-listening, career-oriented female. She was black and she wasn't condescending like so many other staff members were. And when she called him "Jamel," as opposed to "Convict Ross," it made him imagine they had a tighter bond in store.

"So this dude—I won't say his name—he let me in on his check game. He explained how one person could write a check for, say, one hundred grand, give it to a friend, and even if the money isn't there to back up the check, the depositor could likely withdraw money on it before it is found to be worthless. It sounded good. And I figured the worst case scenario would be to deny this and to deny that. . . ."

"They don't verify the check? I mean, isn't that like part of the procedure before it clears?" Kay generally did more talking than this when a convict sat before her. Except she was finding his story, as well as his in-depth knowledge of things, so fascinating.

"See, that's the thing. If the check comes from the same region, or if it's from the other side of the world, it still has to go through a clearinghouse, where all of the checks from *all* of the banks eventually go. So that takes like a couple of days. But banks—certain banks—are on some ol' 'we trust you' stuff, and I guess since they've got your name and address 'n' stuff, they do the cash within one or two days."

"Really?"

"Yup. They will if it's a local check from a local bank. And on that hundred grand? The bank will let loose on the second day. I'll go in and get the money when the dam breaks. . . ."

"And when the bank finds out about the check being no good?"

"I play dumb. I don't know the guy who wrote the check. Met him only twice, blah blah blah. I sign this little BS affidavit and *bang*—I'm knee-deep in free money."

Dr. Kay wagged her head of flowing hair and replied, "You all never cease to amaze me. I mean *you,* as in the convict here. I hear all sorts of tricks and shortcuts and—"

"Cons. They're cons, Doctor Kay."

"Sure, sure . . ." she somehow agreed.

"But it's all a dead-end, ya know? Like, once you get money, it becomes an addiction, to the point that you forget your *reasons* and *objectives* for getting money in the first place."

"Did *you* forget, Jamel?"

"Did I? I got *so deep* in the whole check thing that it became my new profession."

"Stop playin'."

"I'm for real. I started off with my own name and companies, but then, uhh . . ." Jamel hesitated. He looked away from the doctor. "I shouldn't really be tellin' you this. I'm ramblin'."

"You don't have to if you don't want to, but let me remind you that what you say to me in our sessions is confidential, unless I feel that you might cause harm to yourself or someone else, or if I'm subpoenaed to testify in court."

"Hmmm." Jamel deliberated on that. He wondered if the

eighty-four-month sentence could be enhanced to double or triple, or worse. He'd heard about the nightmares, how bragging while in prison was a tool that another prisoner could use to shorten his own sentence. "Informants" they called them. And just the *thought* of that made Jamel promise himself that he wouldn't say a thing about the weapon and the real reason he caught so much time.

"Off the record, Jamel . . ."

"Oooh, I like this 'off-the-record' stuff." Jamel rubbed his hands together and came to the edge of the couch from his slouched position.

"Well, to put your mind at ease, I haven't *yet* received a subpoena for a trial."

Jamel took that as an indication of secrecy and that he was supposed to have confidence in her. But he proceeded with caution as he went on explaining about the various bank scams, the phony licenses and bogus checks.

The doctor said, "Wow, Jamel. That's a hell of a switch. One day you're a television producer, a publisher, and a ladies' man, and the next—"

The phone rang.

"I'm sorry." Dr. Kay got up from her chair, passed Jamel and circled her desk. It gave him a whiff of her perfume, and that only had him pay special attention to her calves. There was something about a woman's calves that got him excited. Or didn't. But Dr. Kay's calves *did*. As she took her phone call, Jamel wondered if she did the StairMaster bit, or if she ran in the mornings. Maybe she was in the military like most of these prison guards claimed. Was she an aerobics instructor at some point in her life? All of those ideas were flowing like sweet Kool-Aid in Jamel's head as he thought and wondered and imagined.

"Could you excuse me?" Dr. Kay said.

"Sure," said Jamel, and he quickly stepped out of the office and shut the door behind him. Through the door's window he tried to cling to her words. It seemed to be a business call, but that was just a guess. A hope. It was part of Jamel's agenda to guess and wonder what this woman or that woman would be like underneath him, or on top of him. After all, he was locked up and unable to touch another being. So, his imaginings were what guided him during these seven years. He'd take time to look deep into a woman, and those thoughts weren't frivolous but anchored and supported by his past. Indeed, sex was a major part of his life from a teen. It had become a part of his lifestyle. Women. The fine ones. The ones who weren't so fine, but whom he felt he could "shape up and get right." Dr. Kay was somewhere in between those images. She had a cute face and an open attitude. Her eyes smiled large and compassionate. She was cheeky when she smiled, with lips wide and supple. Her teeth were bright and indicated good hygiene.

And Dr. Kay wasn't built like an *Essence* model or a dancer in a video. She was a little thick where it mattered, and she had what Jamel considered to be "a lot to work with." Big-breasted with healthy hips, Dr. Kay was one of a half-dozen women on the compound who were black. There were others who were Hispanic and a few more who were white. But of those who were somehow accessible, Dr. Kay nicely fit Jamel's reach. And to reach her, all he had to do was make the effort to trek on down to the psychology department, in the same building as the chapel and the hospital. All you had to do was express interest in counseling. Then you had to pass a litmus test of sorts, giving your reason for needing counseling. Of course, Dr. Kay wasn't the only psychotherapist in the department. There were one or two others. So Jamel had to hope and pray that his interview would 1) be with Dr. Kay Edmonson, and 2) that his address would be taken sincerely, not as just another sex-starved convict who wanted a whiff or an eyeful of the available female on the compound.

Considering all of that, Jamel played his cards right and was always able to have Dr. Kay set him up for a number of appointments. It couldn't be once a week; the doctor-convict relationship would quickly burn out at that rate. But twice a month was a good start, so that she could get a grip on who (and what) he was about. Plus, his visits wouldn't be so obvious as to raise any red flags with her boss, who, as far as Jamel could tell, really didn't execute any major checks and balances of Kay's caseload. Still, it was the other prisoners at Fort Dix who Jamel had to be concerned about. They had to be outsmarted at every twist and turn, since they were the very people (miserable, locked up, and jealous) who would often jump to conclusions. Any one of these guys might get the notion, the hint, or the funny idea that Dr. Kay was getting too personal with one prisoner. Then the dime dropping and the investigation would begin.

HARLEM HEAT

By 50 Cent and Mark Anthony

Fast Forward to:
September 2006
Long Island, New York

I can't front. I was nervous as hell.

My heart was thumping a mile a minute, like it was about to jump outta my chest. The same goddamn state trooper had now been following us for more than three exits and I knew that it was just a matter of seconds before he was gonna turn on his lights and pull us over, so I put on my signal and switched lanes and prepared to exit the parkway, hoping that he would change his mind about stopping us.

"Chyna, what the fuck are you doing?" my moms asked me as she fidgeted in her seat.

"Ma, you know this nigga is gonna pull us over, so I'm just acting like I'm purposely exiting before he pulls us over. It'll be easier to play shit off if he does stop us."

"Chyna, I swear to God you gonna get us locked the fuck up. Just relax and drive!" my mother barked as she turned her head to look in the rearview mirror to confirm that the state trooper was still tailing us. She also reached to turn up the volume on the radio and then slumped in her seat a little bit, trying to relax.

Although my moms was trying to play shit cool, the truth was, I knew that she was just as nervous as I was.

"Ma, I already switched lanes, I gotta get off now or we'll look too suspicious," I explained over the loud R. Kelly and Snoop Dogg song that was coming from the speakers.

As soon as I switched lanes and attempted to make my way to the ramp of exit 13, the state trooper threw on his lights, signaling for me to pull over.

"Ain't this a bitch. Chyna, I told yo' ass."

"Ma, just chill," I barked, cutting my mother off. I was panicking and trying to think fast, and the last thing I needed was for my mother to be bitchin' with me.

"I got this. I'ma pull over and talk us outta this. Just follow my lead," I said with my heart pounding as I exited the parkway ramp and made my way on to Linden Boulevard before bringing the car to a complete stop.

I had my foot on the brake and both of my hands on the steering wheel. I inhaled deeply and then exhaled very visibly before putting the car in park. I quickly exited the car, still wearing my Cartier Aviator gold-rimmed shades to help mask my face. The loud R. Kelly chorus continued playing in the background.

"Officer, I'm sorry if I was speeding, but—"

"Miss, step away from the car and put your hands where I can see them," the lone state trooper shouted at me, interrupting my words. He was clutching the nine-millimeter handgun, still in its holster, and he cautiously approached me. Soon, I no longer heard the music coming from the car and I was guessing that my mother had turned it down so that she could try and listen to what the officer was saying.

"Put my hands on the car for what? Let me just explain where I'm going."

The officer wasn't trying to hear it, and he slammed me up against the hood of the car.

"I got a sick baby in the car. What the hell is wrong with you?" I screamed. I was purposely trying to be dramatic while squirming my body and resisting the officer's efforts to pat me down.

On the inside I was still shitting bricks and my heart was still racing a mile a minute. The car was in park at the side of the road and the engine was running idle. I was hoping that my mom would jump into the driver's seat and speed the hell off. There was no sense in both of us getting bagged. And from the looks of things, the aggressive officer didn't seem like he was in the mood for bullshit.

"Is anyone else in the car with you?" the cop asked me as he felt between my legs up to my crotch, checking for a weapon—though he was clearly feeling for more than just a weapon.

My mother's 745 that I was driving had limousine-style tints, and the state trooper couldn't fully see inside the car.

"Just my moms and my sick baby. Yo, on the real, for real, this is crazy. I ain't even do shit and you got me bent over and slammed up against the hood of the car feeling all on my pussy and shit! I got a sick baby that I'm trying to get to the hospital," I yelled while trying to fast-talk the cop. I sucked my teeth and gave him a bunch of eye-rolling and neck-twisting ghetto attitude.

"You didn't do shit? Well if this is a BMW, then tell me why the fuck your plates are registered to a Honda Accord," the six-foot-four-inch drill-sergeant-looking officer screamed back at me.

The cop then reached to open up the driver's door, and just as he pulled the car door open, my moms opened her passenger door. She hadn't taken off the shades or the hat that she had been wearing, and with one foot on the ground and her other foot still inside the car she stood up and asked across the roof of the car if there was a problem.

"Chyna, you okay? What the fuck is going on, Officer?" my mother asked, sounding as if she was highly annoyed.

"Miss, I need you to step away from the car," the officer shouted at my mother.

"Step away from the car for what?" my moms yelled back with even more disgust in her voice.

"Ma, he on some bullshit, I told him that Nina is in the backseat sick as a damn dog and he still on this ol' racist profiling shit."

As soon as I was done saying those words I heard gunfire erupting.

Blaow. Blaow. Blaow. Blaow.

Instinctively I ducked for cover down near the wheel well, next to the car's twenty-two-inch chrome rims. And when I turned and attempted to see where the shots were coming from, all I saw was the state trooper dropping to the ground. I turned and looked the other way and saw my mom's arms stretched across the roof of the BMW. She was holding her chrome thirty-eight revolver with both hands, ready to squeeze off some more rounds.

"Chyna, you aight?"

"Yeah, I'm good," I shouted back while still half-way crouched down near the tire.

"Well, get your ass in this car and let's bounce!" my moms screamed at me.

I got up off the ground from my kneeling stance and with my high-heeled Bottega Veneta boots I stepped over the bloody state trooper, who wasn't moving. He had been shot point-blank right between the eyes and he didn't look like he was breathing all that well, as blood spilled out of the side of his mouth.

Before I could fully get my ass planted on the cream-colored plush leather driver's seat my mom was hollering for me to hurry up and pull off.

"Drive this bitch, Chyna! I just shot a fucking cop! Drive!"

My mom's frantic yelling had scared my ten-month-old baby, who was strapped in her carseat in the back. So with my moms screaming for me to hurry up and drive away from the crime scene and with my startled baby crying and hitting high notes I put the car in drive and I screeched off, leaving the lifeless cop lying dead in the street.

If shit wasn't thick enough for me and my moms already, killing a state trooper had definitely just made things a whole lot thicker. I sped off doing about sixty miles an hour down a quiet residential street in Elmont, Long Island, just off of Linden Boulevard. My heart was thumping and although it was late afternoon on a bright and sunny summer weekday, I was desperately hoping that no eyewitnesses had seen what went down.

BLOW

by 50 Cent
and K'wan

> **"The game is not for the faint of heart,**
> **and if you choose to play it,**
> **you better damn well understand the rules."**

Prince sat in the stiff wooden chair totally numb. The tailored Armani suit he had been so proud of when he dropped two grand on it now felt like a straitjacket. He spared a glance at his lawyer who was going over his notes with a worried expression on his face. The young black man had fought the good fight, but in the end it would be in God's hands.

He tried to keep from looking over his shoulder, but he couldn't help it. There was no sign of Sticks, which didn't surprise him. For killing a police officer they were surely going to give him the needle, if he even survived being captured. The police had dragged the river but never found a body. Everyone thought Sticks was dead, but Stone said otherwise. Sticks was his twin, and he would know better than anyone else if he was gone. Prince hoped that Stone was right and wished his friend well wherever fate carried him.

Marisol sat two rows behind him, with Mommy at her side looking every bit of the concerned grandmother. It was hard to believe that she was the embodiment of death, cloaked in kindness. This was the first time he had seen Mommy since his incarceration, but Marisol had been there every day for the seven weeks the trial had gone on. She tried to stay strong for her man, but he could tell that the ordeal was breaking her down. Cano had sent word through her that he would be taken care of, but Prince didn't want to be taken care of; he wanted to be free.

Keisha sat in the last row, quietly sobbing. She had raised the most hell when the bulls hit, even managing to get herself tossed into jail for obstruction of justice. She had always been a down bitch, and he respected her for it.

Assembled in the courtroom were many faces. Some were friends, but most were people from the neighborhood that just came to be nosey. No matter their motive the sheer number would look good on his part in the eyes of the jury, at least that was what his lawyer had told him. The way the trial seemed to be going, he seriously doubted it at that point.

Lined up to his left were his longtime friends, Daddy-O and Stone. Daddy-O's face was solemn. His dress shirt was pinned up at the shoulder covering the stump where his left arm used to be. It was just one more debt that he owed Diego that he'd never be able to collect on. Stone smirked at a doodling he had done on his legal pad. Prince wasn't sure if he didn't understand the charges they were facing or just didn't care. Knowing Stone, it was probably the latter. He had long ago resigned himself to the fact that he was born into the game and would die in it.

Prince wanted to break down every time he thought how his run as a boss had ended. To see men that you had grown to love like family take the stand and try to snatch your life to save their own was a feeling that he wouldn't wish on anyone. *No man above the team* was the vow that they had all taken, but in the end only a few kept to it. To the rest, they were just words. They had laughed, cried, smoked weed, and got pussy together, but when the time came to stand like men they laid down like bitches. These men had been like his brothers, but that was before the money came into the picture.

CHAPTER 1
6 months earlier

"Come on Daddy-O, you know me." The young man reminded him, not believing that he'd been turned down. He could already feel the sweat trickling down his back and didn't know how much longer he could hold out.

Daddy-O popped a handful of sunflower seeds in his mouth. He expertly extracted the seeds using only his tongue and let the shells tumble around in his mouth until he could feel the salty bite. "My dude, why are you even talking to me about this; holla at my young boy." He nodded at Danny.

"Daddy, you know how this little nigga is; he wouldn't let his mama go for a short, so you know I ain't getting a play."

"Get yo money right and we won't have a problem," Danny told him, and went back to watching the block.

"Listen," the young man turned back to Daddy-O. A thin film of sweat had begun to form on his nose. "All I got is ten dollars on me, but I need at least two to get me to the social security building in the morning. Do me this solid, and I swear I'll get you right when my check comes through."

Daddy-O looked over at Danny, who was giving the kid the once-over. He was short and thin with braids that snaked down the back of his neck. Danny had one of those funny faces. It was kind of like he looked old, but young at the same time . . . if that makes sense.

There was a time when Danny seemed like he had a bright future ahead of him. Though he wasn't the smartest of their little unit, he was a natural at sports. Danny played basketball for Cardinal Hayes High School and was one of the better players on the team. His jump shot needed a little fine-tuning, but he had a mean handle. Danny was notorious for embarrassing his opponents with his wicked crossover. Sports was supposed to be Danny's ticket out, but as most naïve young men did, he chose Hell over Heaven.

For as talented as Danny was physically, he was borderline retarded mentally. Of course not in a literal sense, but his actions made him the most dim-witted of the crew. While his school chums were content to play the role of gangstas and watch the game from afar, Danny had to be in the thick of it. It was his fascination with the game that caused him to drop out of school in his senior year to pursue his dreams of being a *real nigga*, or a real nigga's sidekick. Danny was a yes-man to the boss, and under the boss is where he would earn his stripes. He didn't really have the heart of a soldier, but he was connected to some stand-up dudes, which provided him with a veil of protection. The hood knew that if you fucked with Danny, you'd have to fuck with his team.

"Give it to him, D," Daddy-O finally said.

Danny looked like he wanted to say something, but a stern look from Daddy-O hushed him. Dipping his hand into the back of his pants, Danny fished around until he found what he was looking for. Grumbling, he handed the young man a small bag of crack.

The young man examined the bag and saw that it was mostly flake and powder. "Man, this ain't nothing but some shake."

"Beggars can't be choosers; take that shit and bounce," Danny spat.

"Yo, shorty you be on some bullshit," the young man said to Danny. There was a hint of anger in his voice, but he knew better than to get stupid. "One day you're gonna have to come from behind Prince and Daddy-O's skirts and handle your own business."

"Go ahead wit that shit, man," Daddy-O said, cracking another seed.

"No disrespect to you, Daddy-O, but shorty got a big mouth. He be coming at niggaz sideways, and it's only on the strength of y'all that nobody ain't rocked him yet."

"Yo, go head wit all that *rocking* shit, niggaz know where I be," Danny said, trying to sound confident. In all truthfulness, he was nervous. He loved the rush of being in the hood with Daddy-O and the team, but didn't care for the bullshit that came with it. Anybody who's ever spent a day on the streets knows that the law of the land more often than not is violence. If you weren't ready to defend your claim, then you needed to be in the house watching UPN.

The young man's eyes burned into Danny's. "Ima see you later," he said, never taking his eyes off Danny as he backed away.

"I'll be right here," Danny said confidently. His voice was deep and stern, but his legs felt like spaghetti. If the kid had rushed him, Danny would have had no idea what to do. He would fight if forced, but it wasn't his first course of action. Only when the kid had disappeared down the path did he finally force himself to relax.

"Punk-ass nigga," Danny said, like he was 'bout that.

"Yo, why you always acting up?" Daddy-O asked.

"What you mean, son?" Danny replied, as if he hadn't just clowned the dude.

"Every time I turn around your ass is in some shit, and that ain't what's up."

Danny sucked his teeth. "Yo, son was trying to stunt on me, B. You know I can't have niggaz coming at my head that way."

"Coming at your head?" Daddy-O raised his eyebrow. "Nigga, he was short two dollars!"

"I'm saying . . ."

"Don't say nothing," Daddy-O cut him off. "We out here trying to get a dollar and you still on your schoolyard bullshit. You

need to respect these streets if you gonna get money in them."
Daddy-O stormed off leaving Danny there to ponder what he had
said.

■

The intense heat from the night before had spilled over to join
with the morning sun and punish anyone who didn't have air-
conditioning, which amounted to damn near the whole hood being outside. That morning the projects were a kaleidoscope of
activity. People were drinking, having water fights, and just trying to sit as still as they could in the heat. Grills were set up in
front of several buildings, sending smoke signals to the hungry
inhabitants.

Daddy-O bopped across the courtyard between 875 and 865.
He nodded to a few heads as he passed them, but didn't really
stop to chat. It was too damn hot, and being a combination of fat
and black made you a target for the sun's taunting rays. A girl
wearing boy shorts and a tank top sat on the bench enjoying an
ice-cream cone. She peeked at Daddy-O from behind her pink
sunglasses and drew the tip of her tongue across the top of the ice
cream.

"Umm, hmm," Daddy-O grumbled, rubbing his large belly. In
the way of being attractive, Daddy-O wasn't much to look at. He
was a five-eight brute with gorilla-like arms and a jaw that looked
to be carved from stone. Cornrows snaked back over his large
head and stopped just behind his ears. Though some joked that he

had a face that only a mother could love, Daddy-O had swagger. His gear was always up, and he was swift with the gift of gab, earning him points with the ladies.

Everybody in the hood knew Daddy-O. He had lived in the Frederick Douglass Houses for over twelve years at that point. He and his mother had moved there when he was seven years old. Daddy-O had lived a number of places in his life, but no place ever felt like Douglass.

Daddy-O was about to head down the stairs toward 845 when he heard his name being called. He slowed, but didn't stop walking as he turned around. Shambling from 875 in his direction was a crackhead that they all knew as Shakes. She tried to strut in her faded high-heeled shoes, but it ended up as more of a walk-stumble. She was dressed in a black leotard that looked like it was crushing her small breasts. Shakes had been a'ight back in her day, but she didn't get the memo that losing eighty pounds and most of your front teeth killed your sex appeal.

"Daddy-O, let me holla at you for a minute," she half slurred. Shakes's eyes were wide and constantly scanning as if she was expecting someone to jump out on her. She stepped next to Daddy-O and whispered in his ear, "You holding?"

"You know better than that, ma. Go see my little man in the building," he said, in a pleasant tone. Most of the dealers in the neighborhood saw the crackheads as being something less than human and treated them as such, but not Daddy-O. Having watched his older brother and several of his other relatives succumb to one drug or another, Daddy-O understood it better than most. Cocaine and heroin were the elite of their line. Boy and Girl, as they were sometimes called, were God and Goddess to those foolish enough to be enticed by their lies. They had had the highest addiction rate, and the most cases of relapses. Daddy-O had learned early that a well-known crackhead could be more valuable to you than a member of your team, if you knew how to use them.

"A'ight, baby, that's what it is," she turned to walk away and almost lost her balance. In true crackhead form, she righted herself and tried to strut even harder. "You need to call a sista sometime," she called over her shoulder.

Daddy-O shook his head. There wasn't a damn thing he could call Shakes but what she was, a corpse that didn't know it was dead yet. Daddy-O continued down the stairs and past the small playground. A group of kids were dancing around in the elephant-shaped sprinkler tossing water on each other. One of them ran up on Daddy-O with a half-filled bowl, but a quick threat of an ass whipping sent the kid back to douse one of his friends with the water. Stopping to exchange greetings with a Puerto Rican girl he knew, Daddy-O disappeared inside the bowels of 845.